# SERVICE PUPS in Training

# ELLIE'S BRAVE SEARCH
## A Search and Rescue Dog Graphic Novel

written by Mari Bolte    illustrated by Diego Vaisberg

PICTURE WINDOW BOOKS
a capstone imprint

Published by Picture Window Books, an imprint of Capstone
1710 Roe Crest Drive, North Mankato, Minnesota 56003
www.capstonepub.com

**Library of Congress Cataloging-in-Publication Data**
ISBN: 9781484680261 (hardcover)
ISBN: 9781484680216 (paperback)
ISBN: 9781484680223 (ebook PDF)

Summary: Ellie, a bloodhound puppy, starts training to
become a search and rescue dog.

**Editorial Credits**
Editor: Christianne Jones; Designer: Elyse White;
Media Researcher: Rebekah Hubstenberger;
Production Specialist: Whitney Schaefer

**Image and Design Credits**
Getty Images: TerryJ, 30; Shutterstock: minizen,
design element (bone icon)

Printed and bound in China. 5557

# Meet

## Ellie

Ellie is a bloodhound puppy. She's training to be a search and rescue (SAR) dog. All the dogs in her family have proven themselves as great SAR dogs. Bloodhounds have sensitive noses. Their ears drag on the ground and help them detect scents too. Ellie likes eating dog ice cream and digging holes.

# How to Read a GRAPHIC NOVEL

Graphic novels are easy to read. Boxes called panels show you how to follow the story. Look at the panels from left to right and top to bottom.

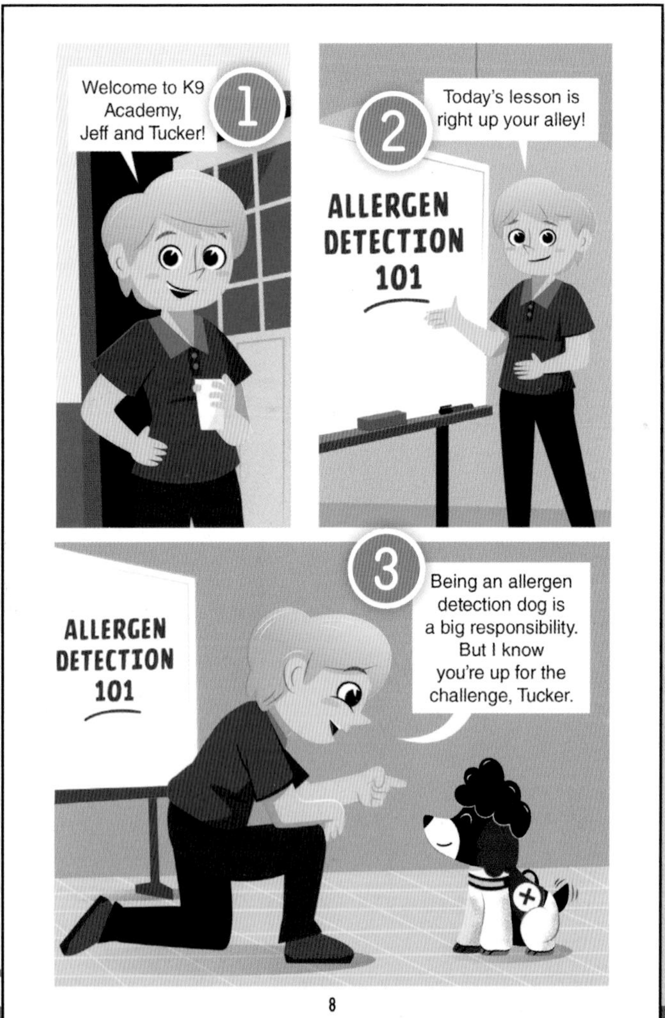

1
Welcome to K9 Academy, Jeff and Tucker!
2
Today's lesson is right up your alley!
ALLERGEN DETECTION 101
3
Being an allergen detection dog is a big responsibility. But I know you're up for the challenge, Tucker.
ALLERGEN DETECTION 101

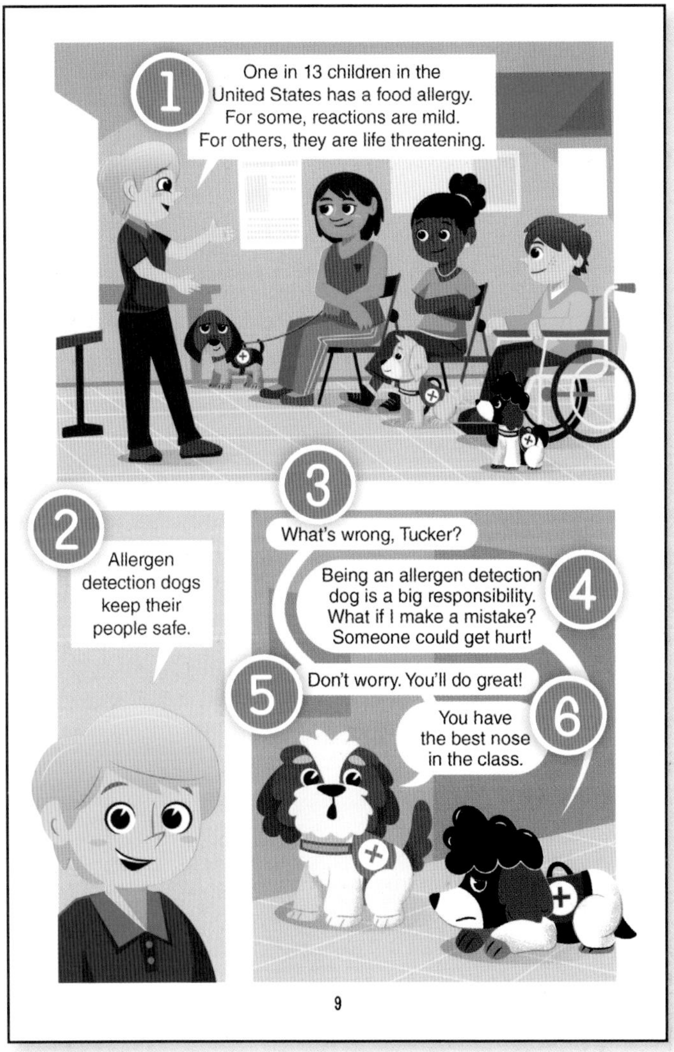
1
One in 13 children in the United States has a food allergy. For some, reactions are mild. For others, they are life threatening.
2
Allergen detection dogs keep their people safe.
3
What's wrong, Tucker?
4
Being an allergen detection dog is a big responsibility. What if I make a mistake? Someone could get hurt!
5
Don't worry. You'll do great!
6
You have the best nose in the class.
9

Read the word boxes and word balloons from left to right as well. Don't forget the sound and action words in the pictures. The pictures and the words work together to tell the whole story.

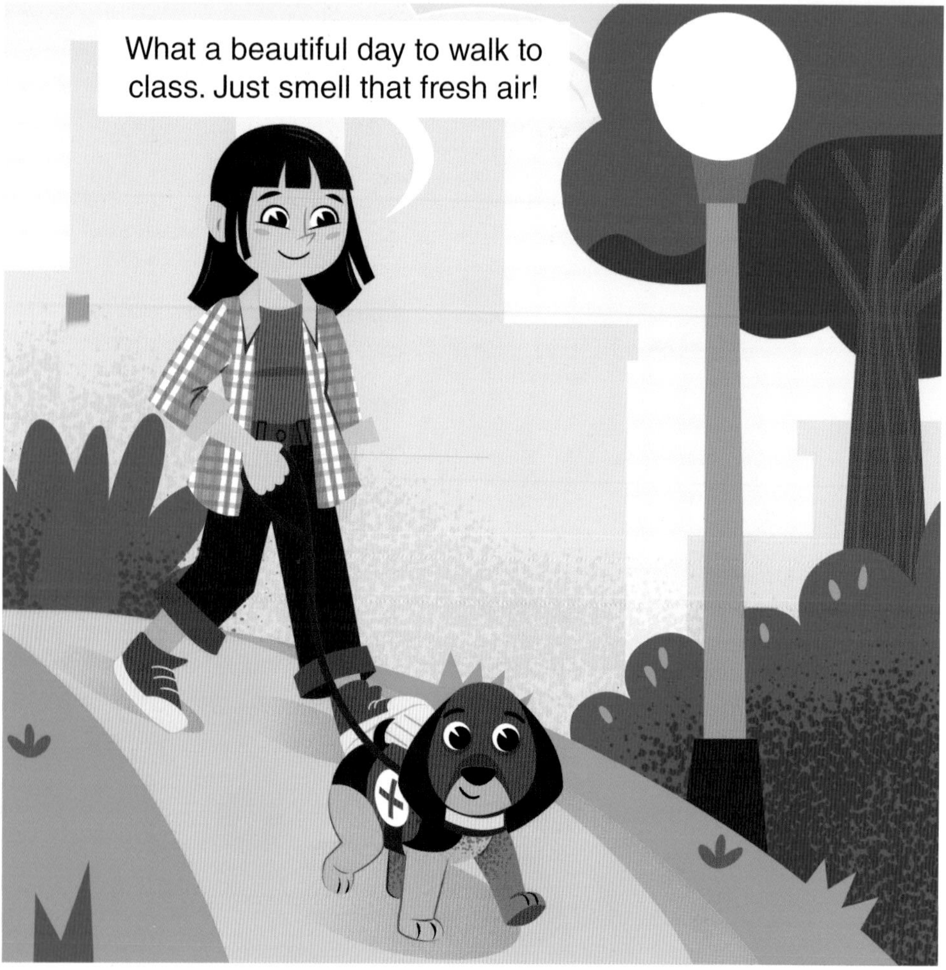
What a beautiful day to walk to class. Just smell that fresh air!

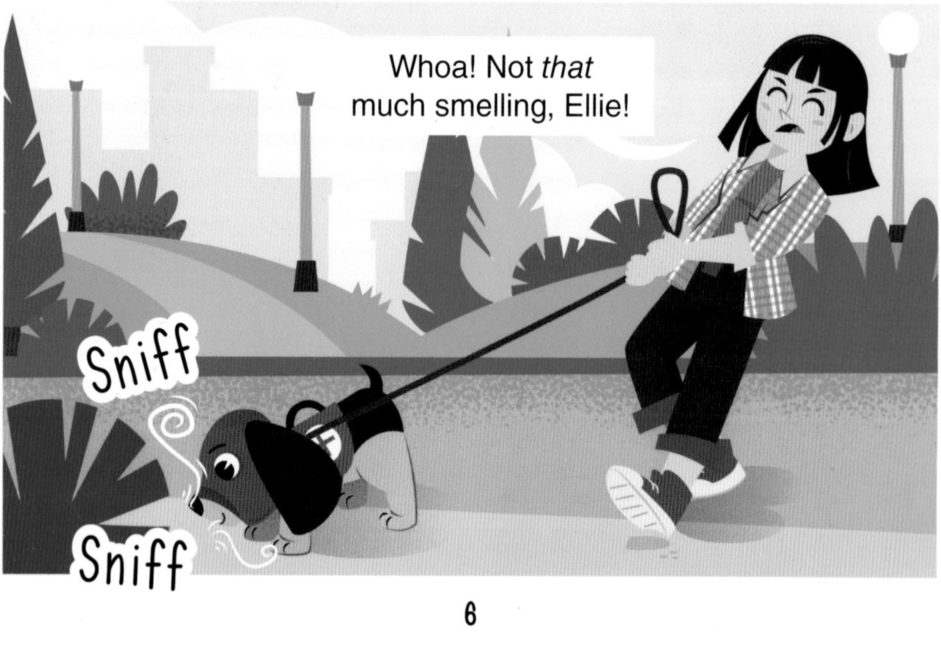
Whoa! Not *that* much smelling, Ellie!
Sniff
Sniff

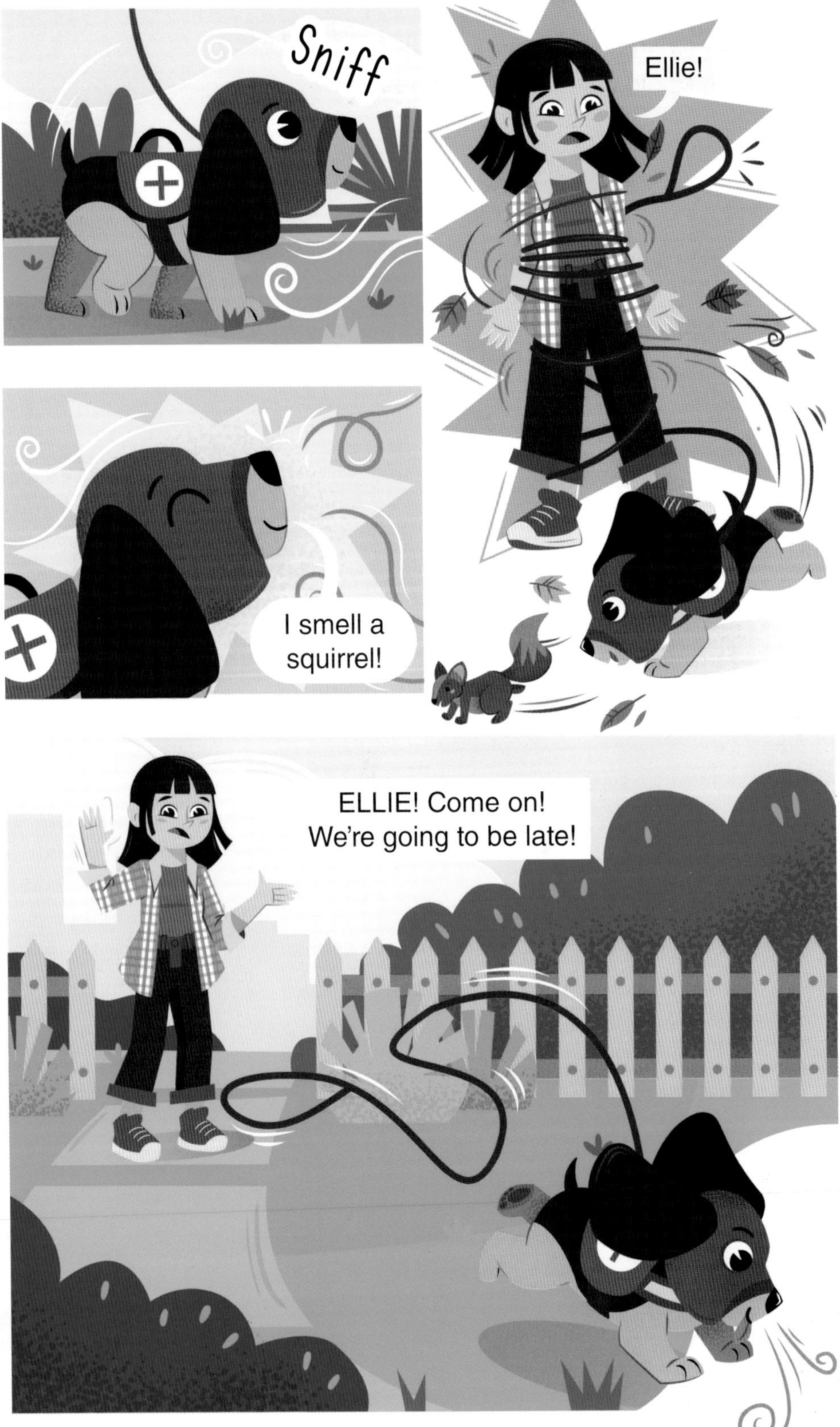
Sniff
Ellie!
I smell a squirrel!
ELLIE! Come on! We're going to be late!

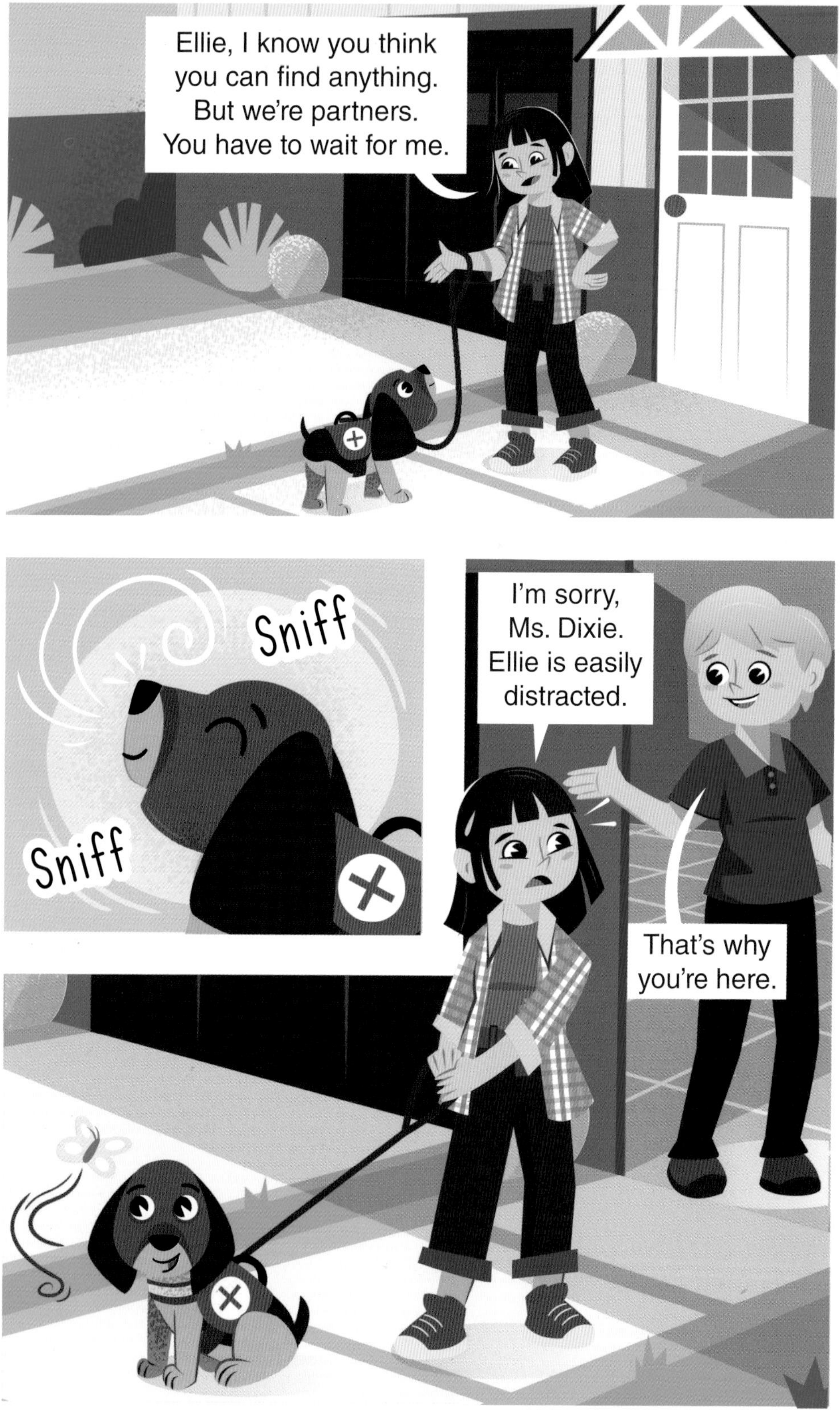
Ellie, I know you think you can find anything. But we're partners. You have to wait for me.
Sniff
Sniff
I'm sorry, Ms. Dixie. Ellie is easily distracted.
That's why you're here.

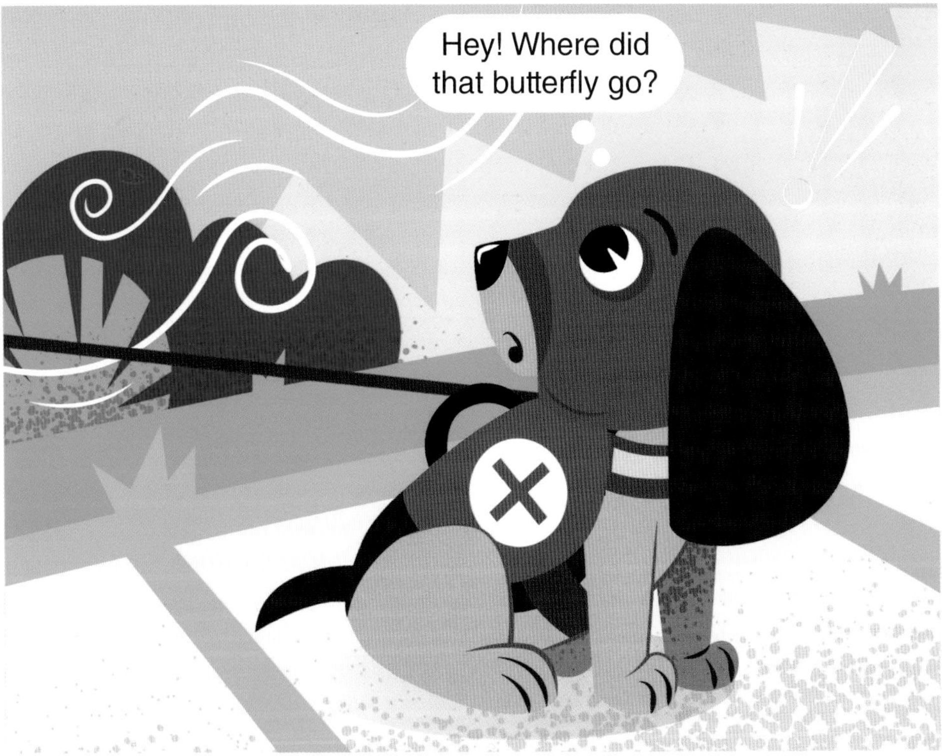
Hey! Where did that butterfly go?

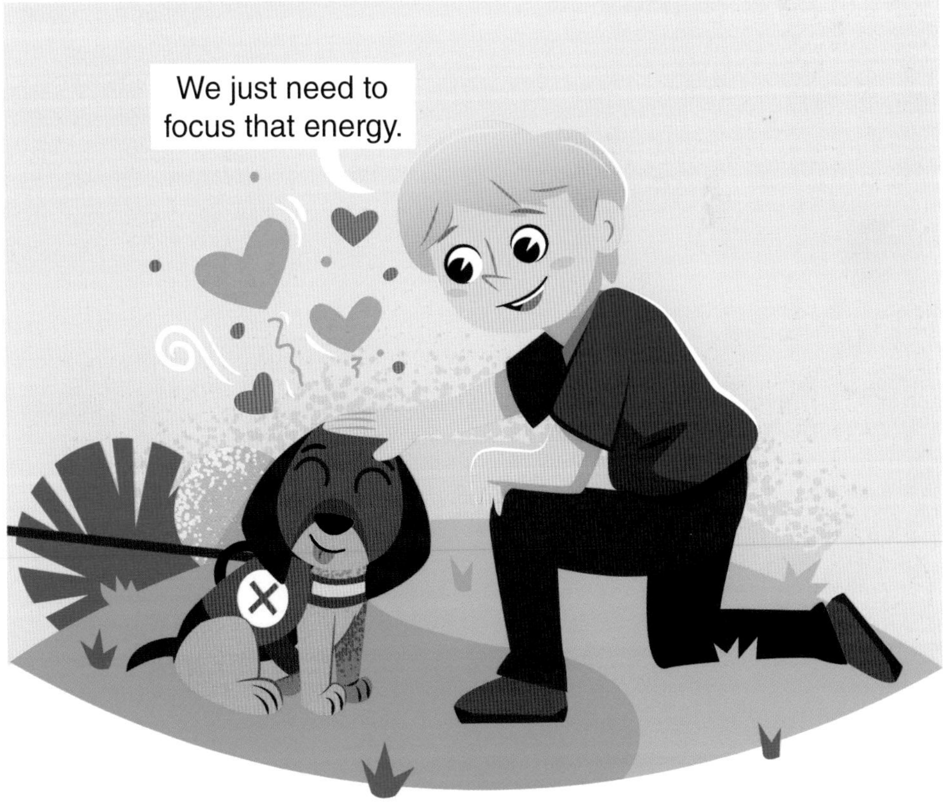
We just need to focus that energy.

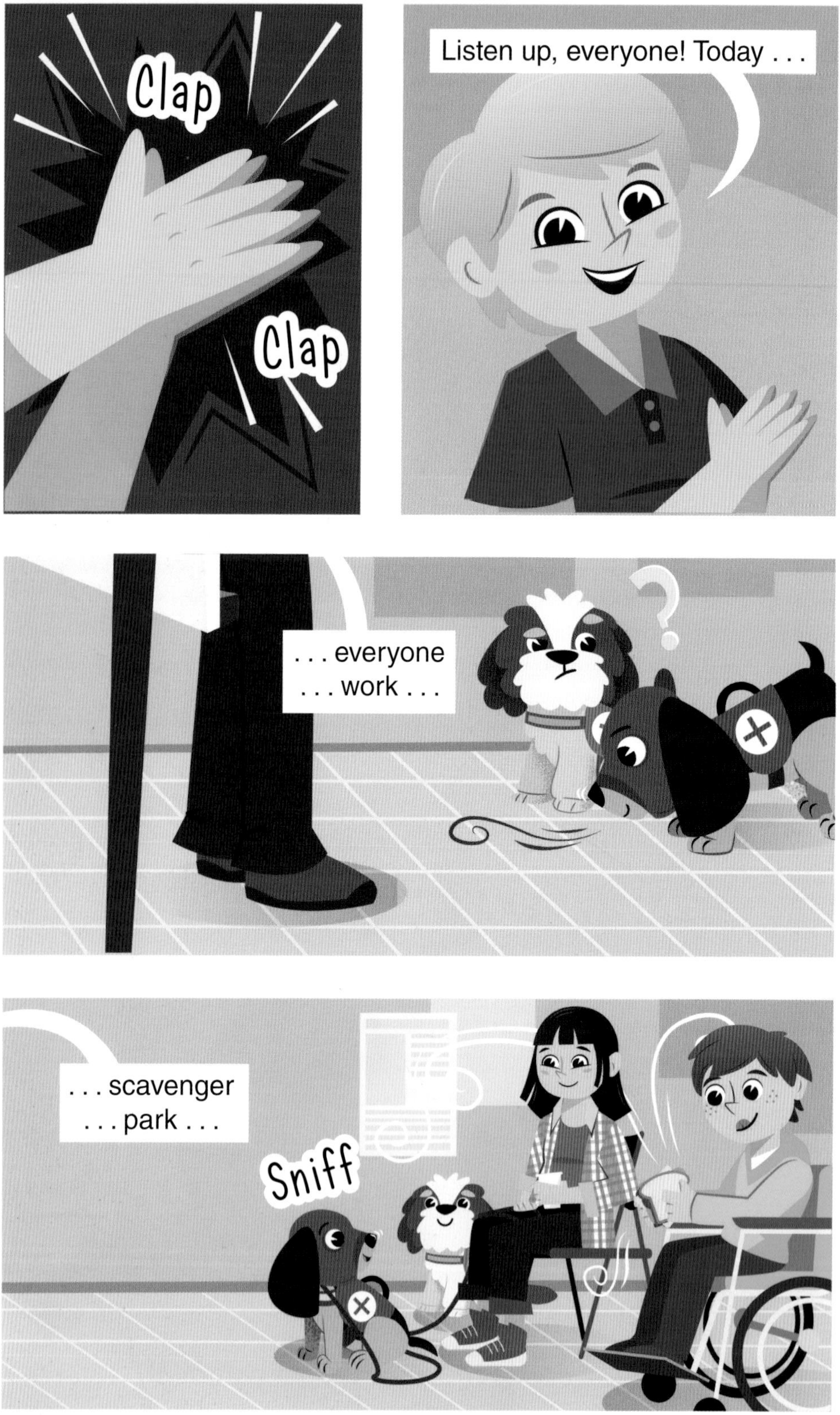
Clap
Clap
Listen up, everyone! Today . . .
. . . everyone
. . . work . . .
. . . scavenger
. . . park . . .
Sniff

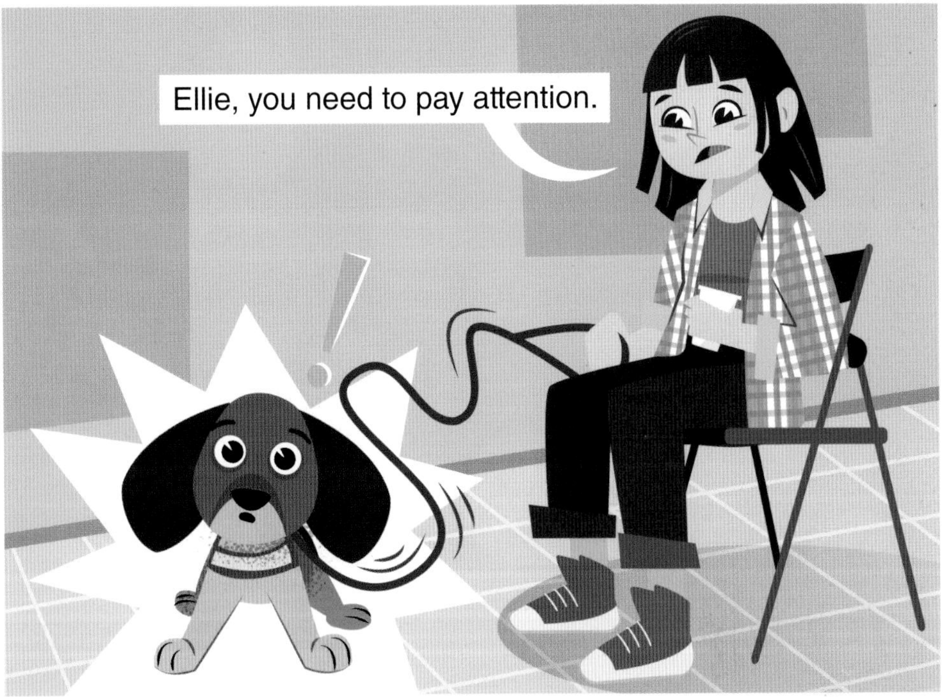
Ellie, you need to pay attention.

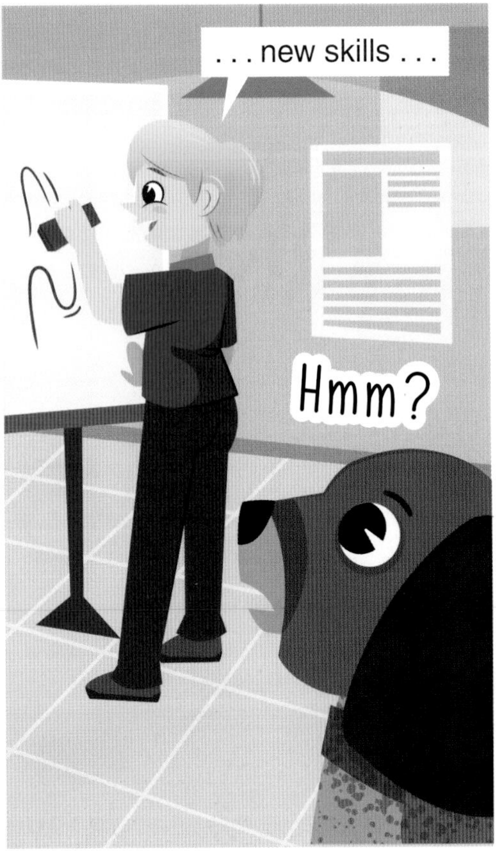
. . . new skills . . .
Hmm?

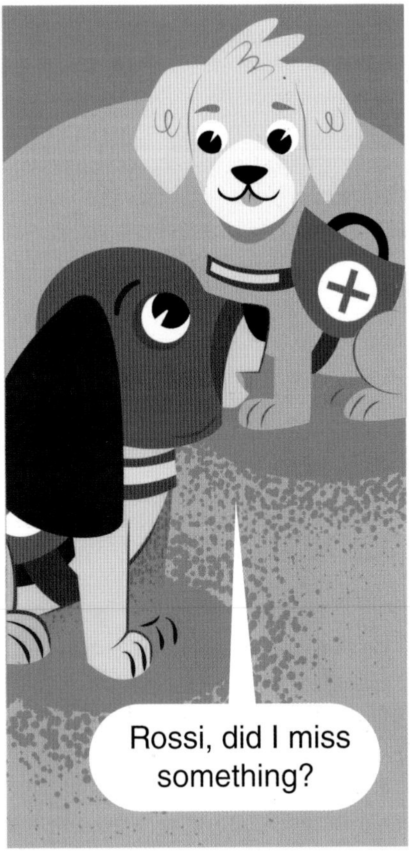
Rossi, did I miss something?

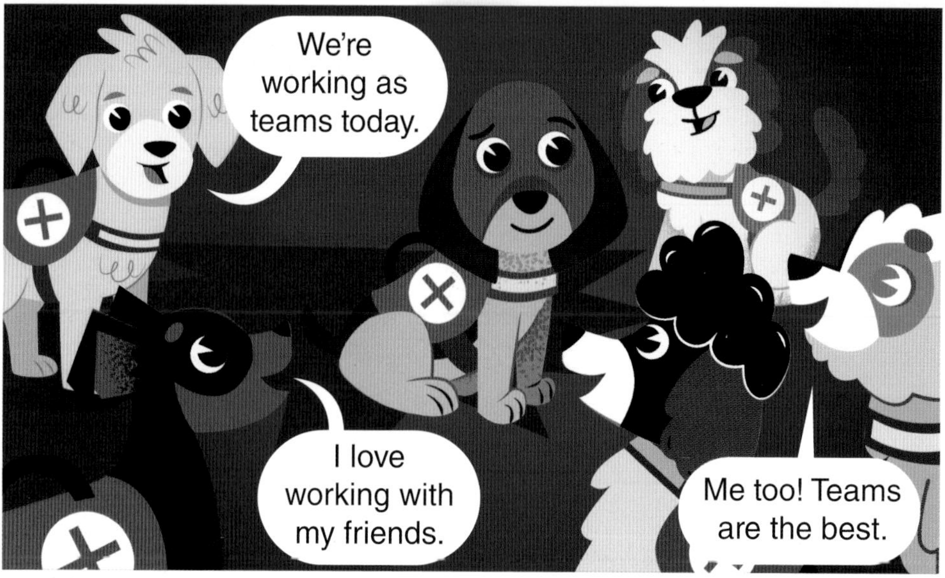
We're working as teams today.
I love working with my friends.
Me too! Teams are the best.

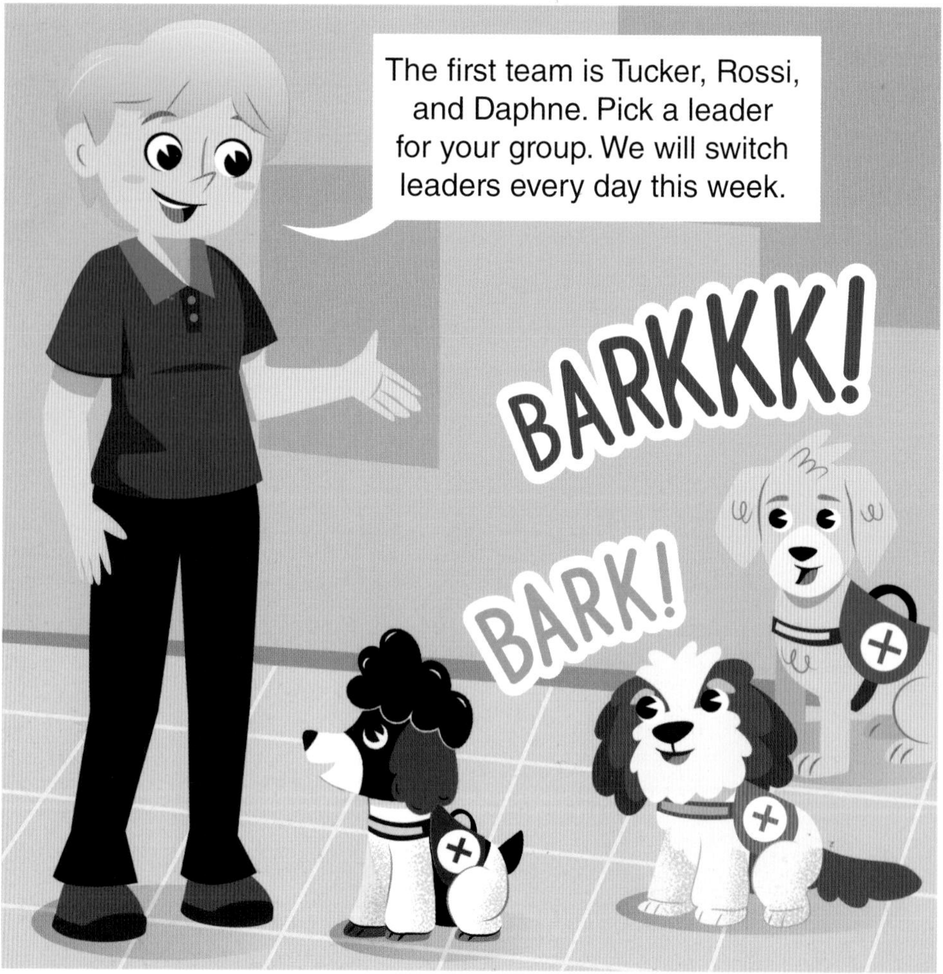
The first team is Tucker, Rossi, and Daphne. Pick a leader for your group. We will switch leaders every day this week.
BARKKK!
BARK!

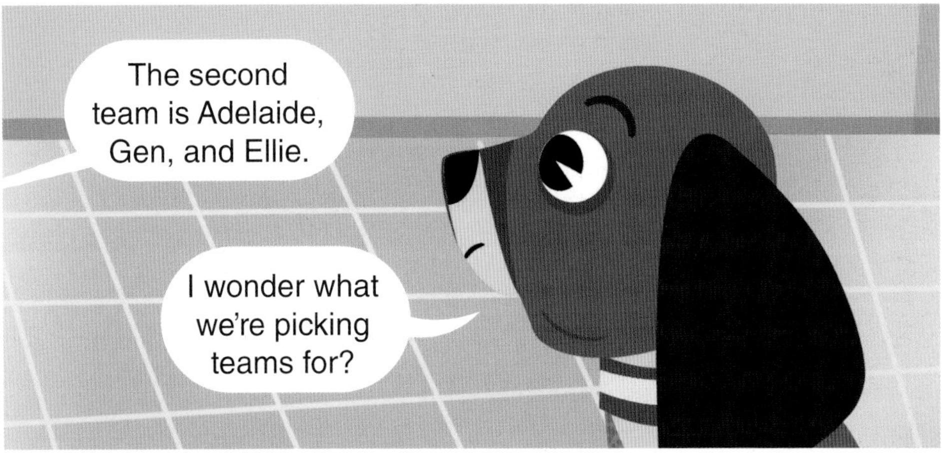
The second team is Adelaide, Gen, and Ellie.
I wonder what we're picking teams for?

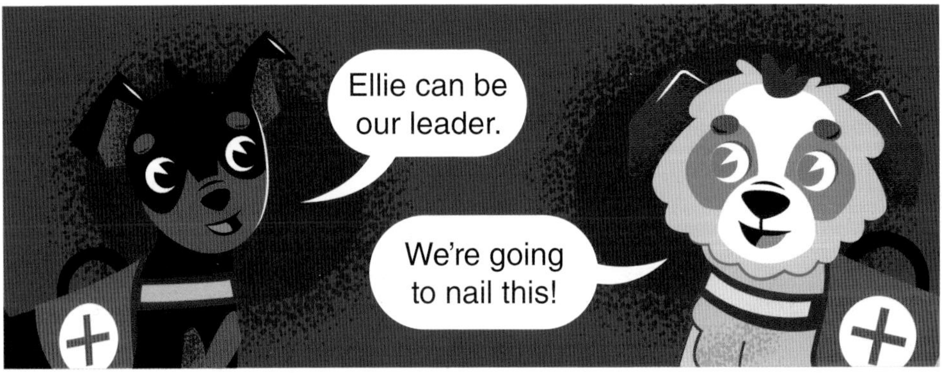
Ellie can be our leader.
We're going to nail this!

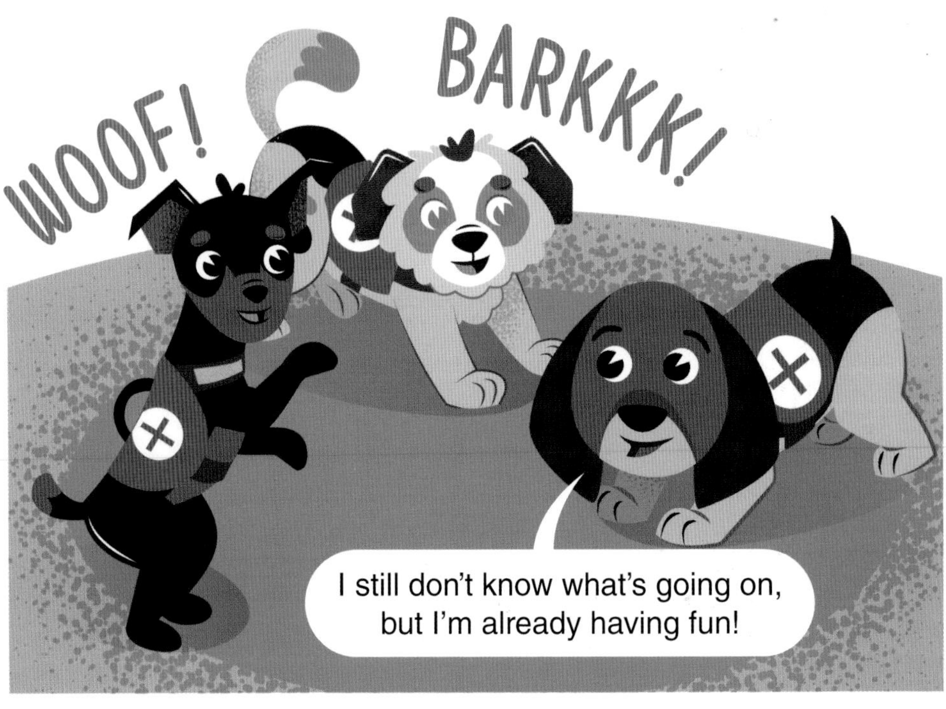
WOOF!
BARKKK!
I still don't know what's going on, but I'm already having fun!

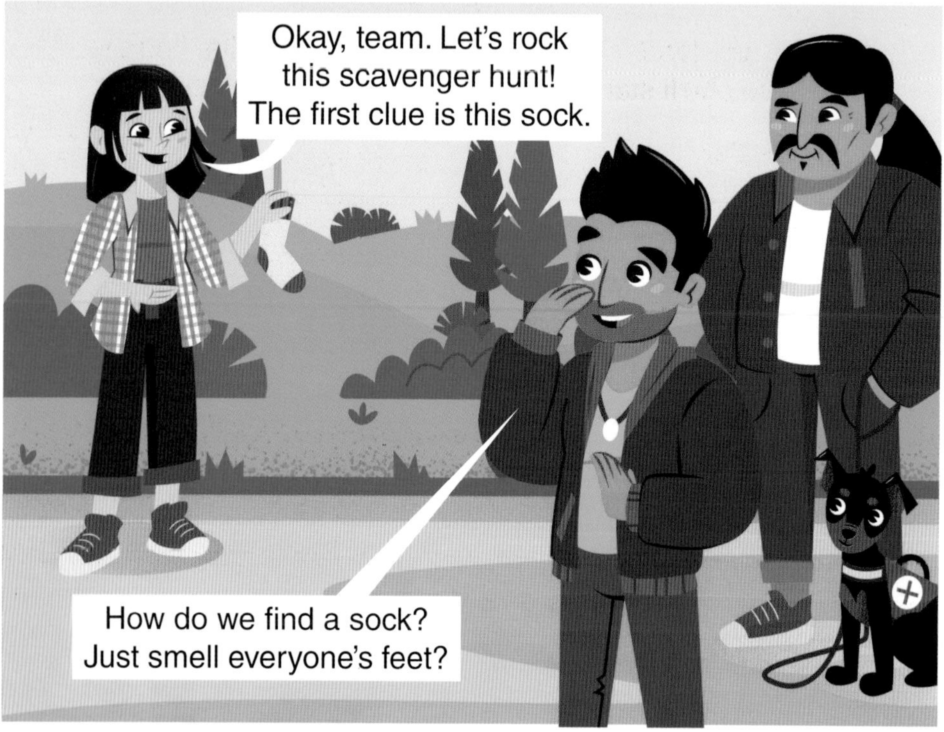
Okay, team. Let's rock this scavenger hunt! The first clue is this sock.
How do we find a sock? Just smell everyone's feet?

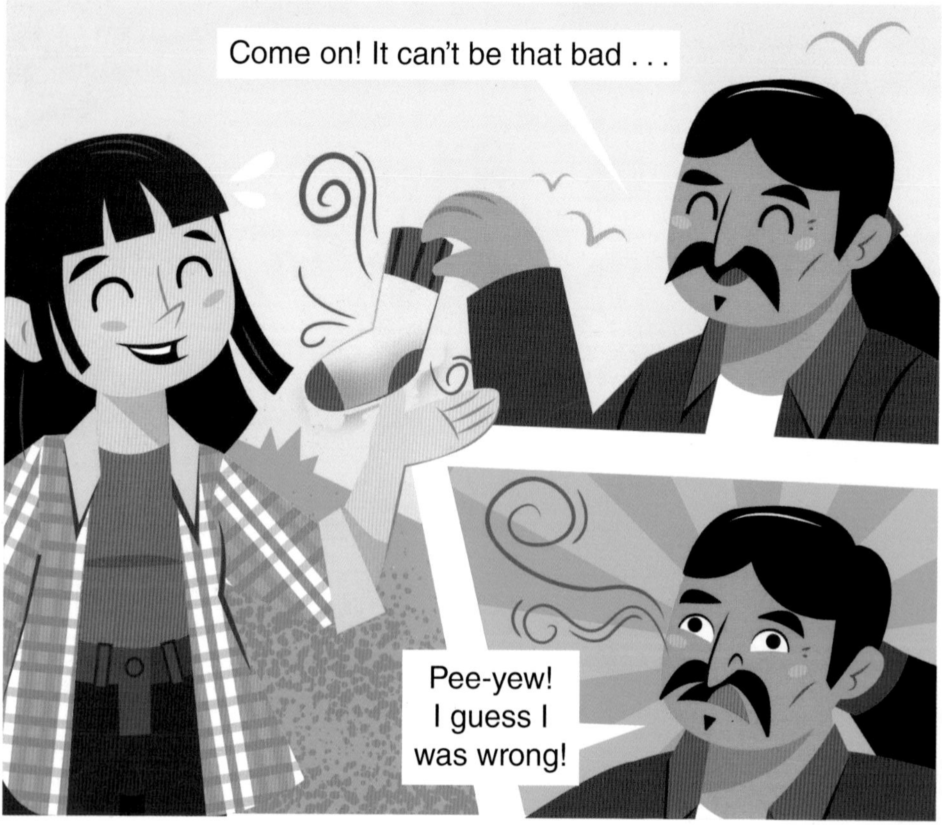
Come on! It can't be that bad . . .
Pee-yew! I guess I was wrong!

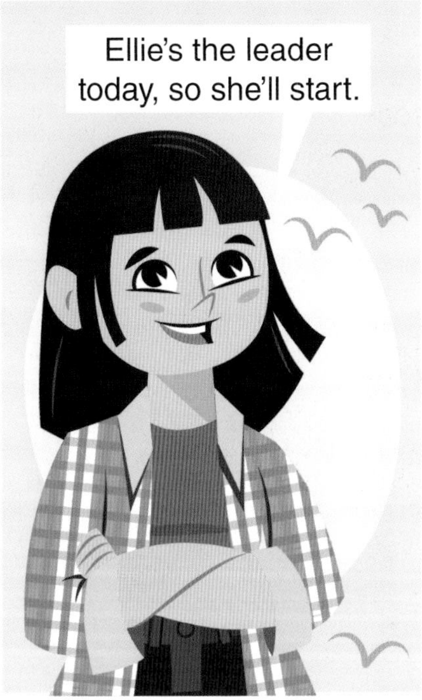
Ellie's the leader today, so she'll start.

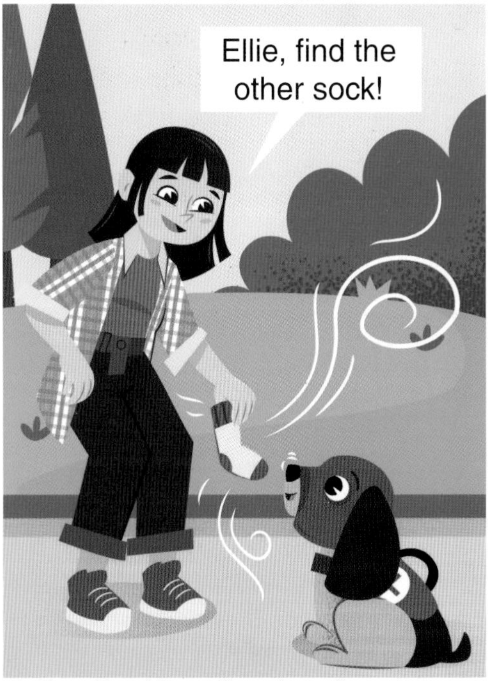
Ellie, find the other sock!

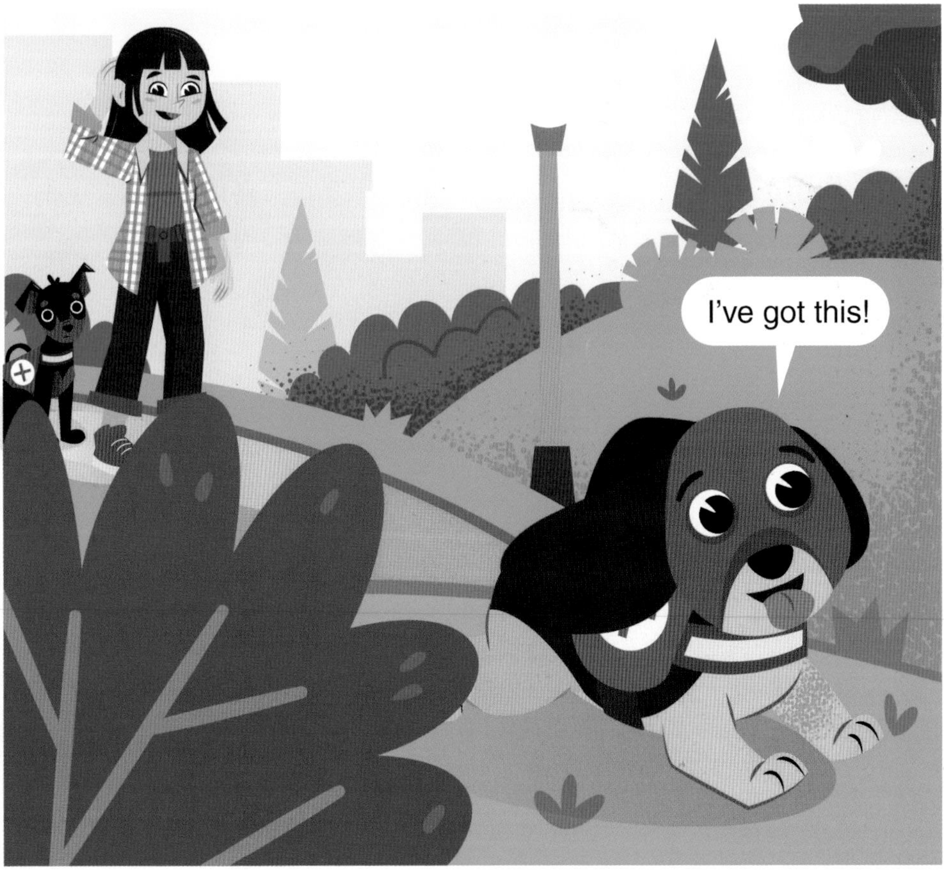
I've got this!

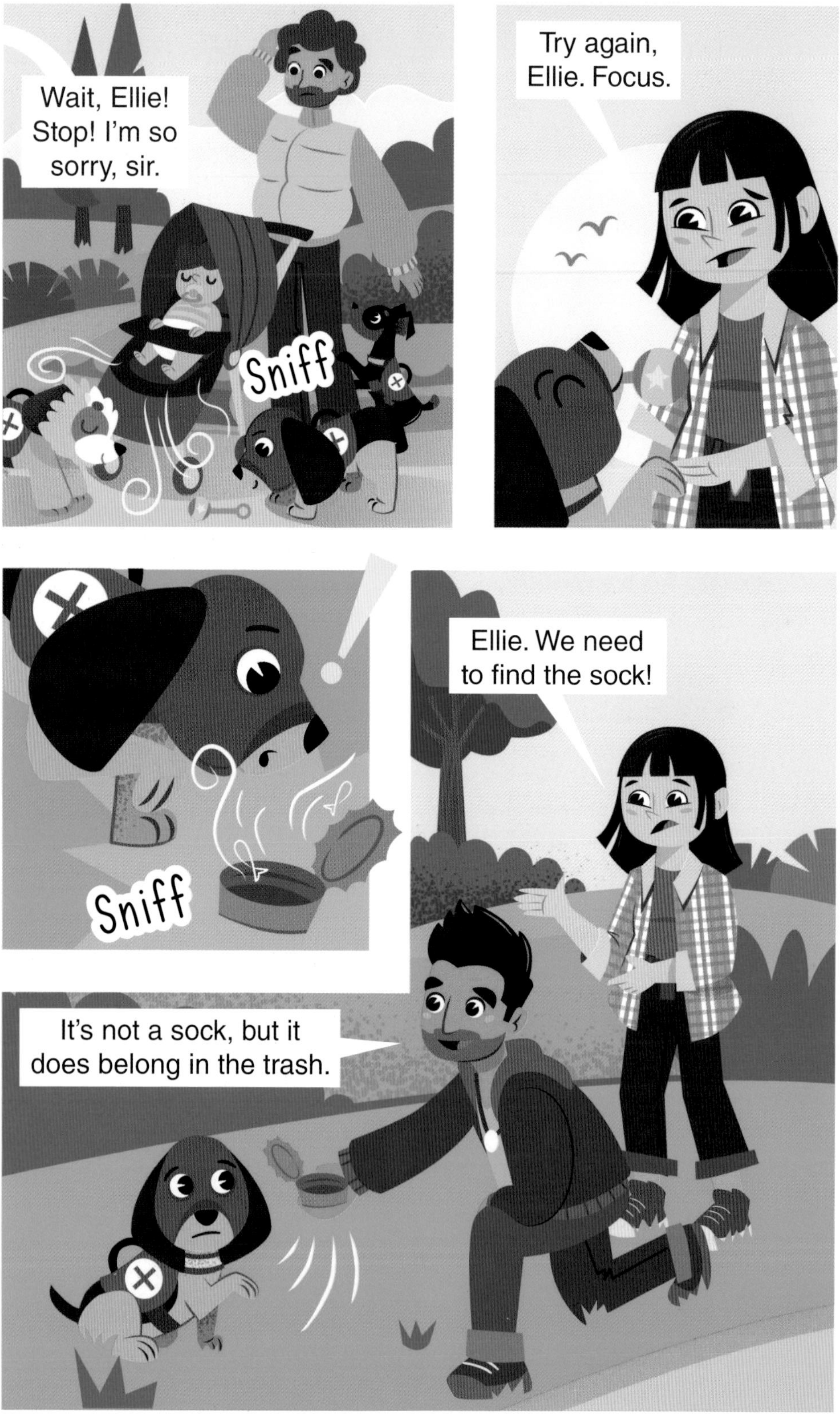
Wait, Ellie! Stop! I'm so sorry, sir.
Sniff
Try again, Ellie. Focus.
Sniff
Ellie. We need to find the sock!
It's not a sock, but it does belong in the trash.

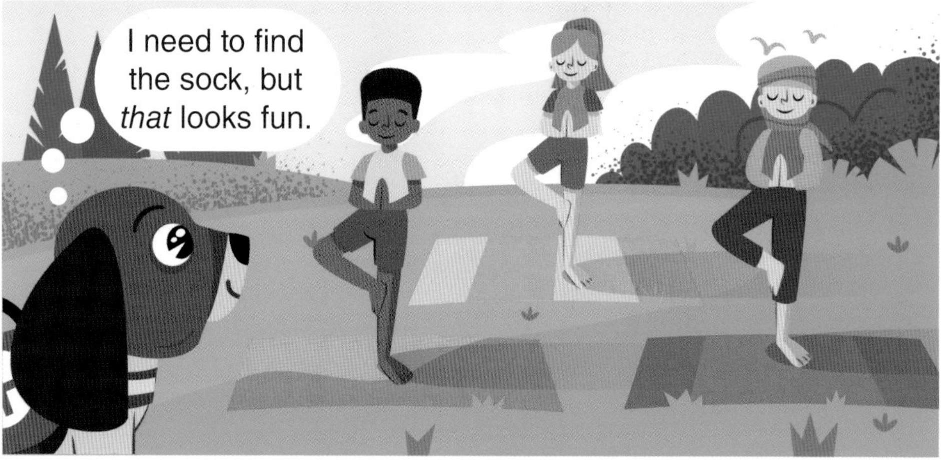
I need to find the sock, but *that* looks fun.

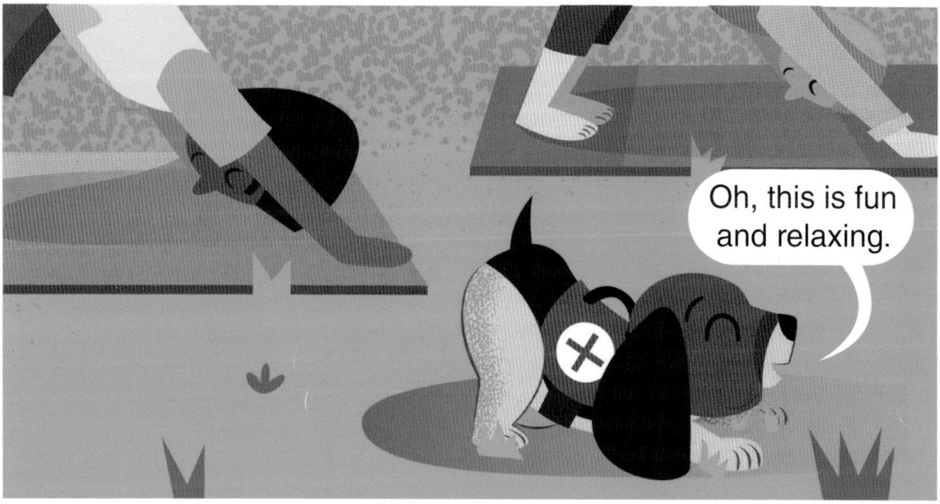
Oh, this is fun and relaxing.

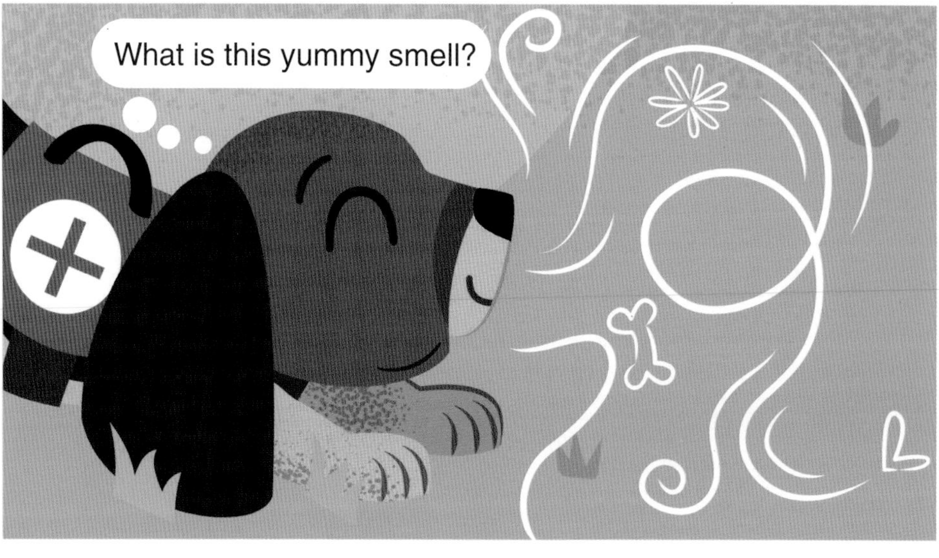
What is this yummy smell?

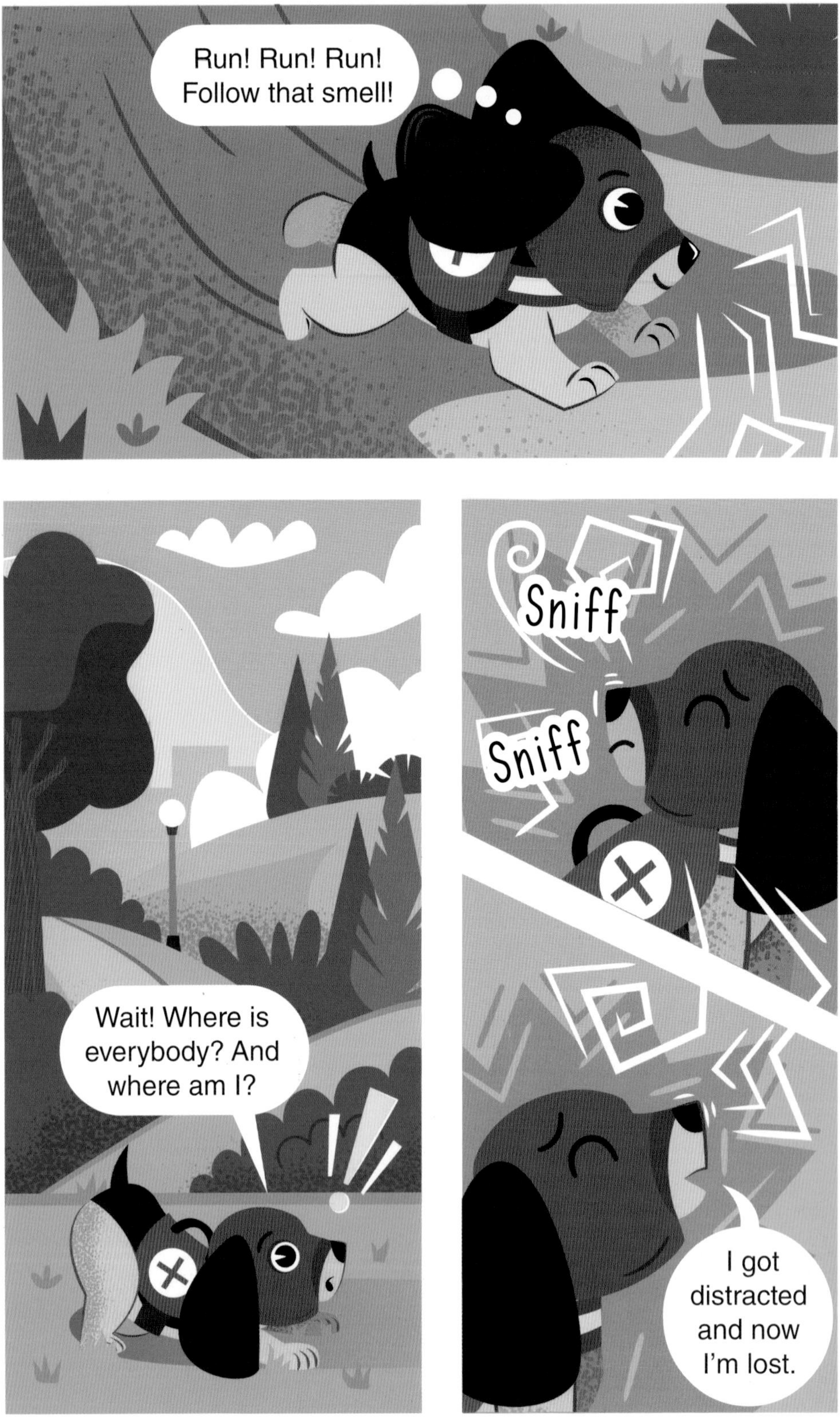
Run! Run! Run! Follow that smell!
Wait! Where is everybody? And where am I?
Sniff
Sniff
I got distracted and now I'm lost.

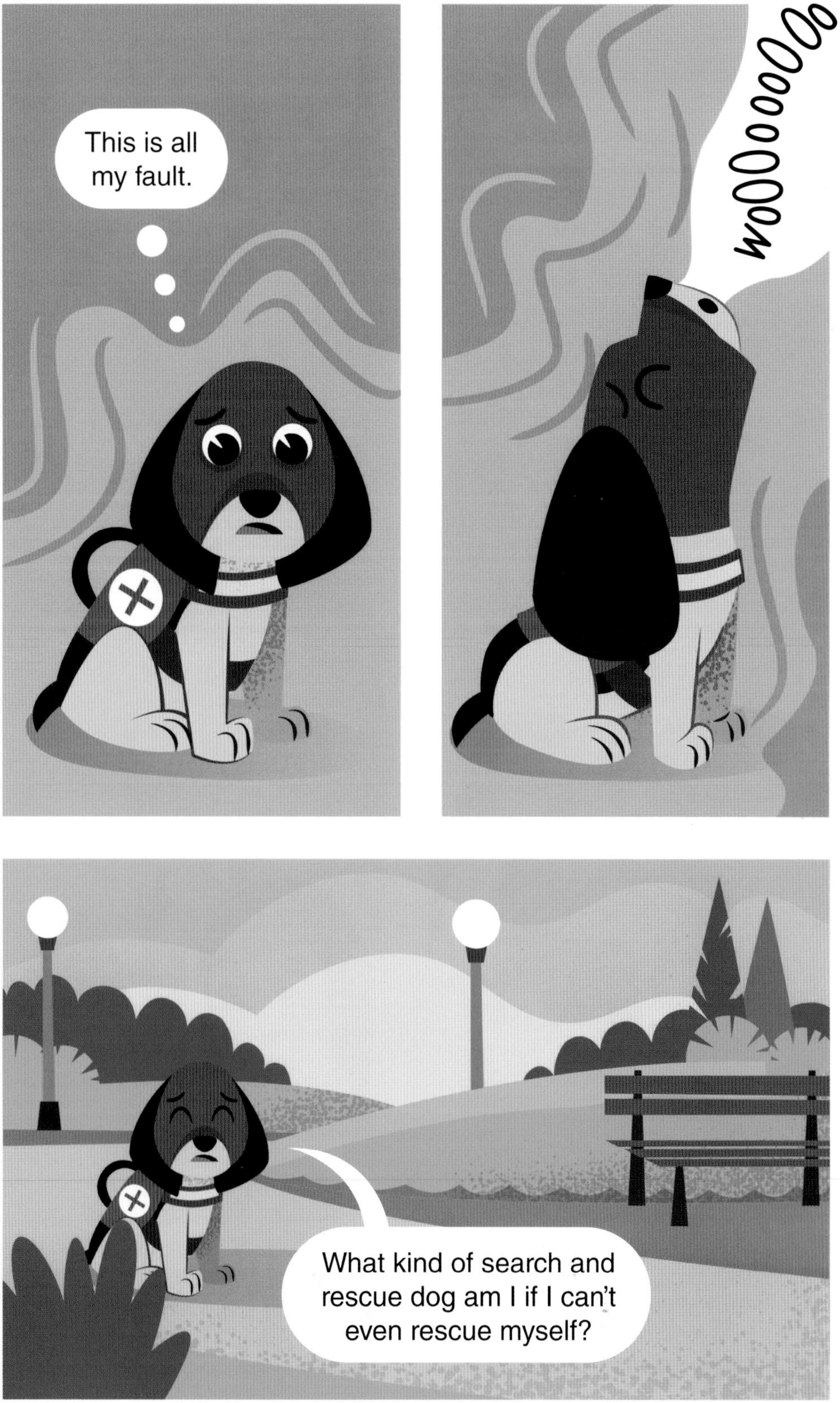
This is all my fault.
wOOoooOOo
What kind of search and rescue dog am I if I can't even rescue myself?

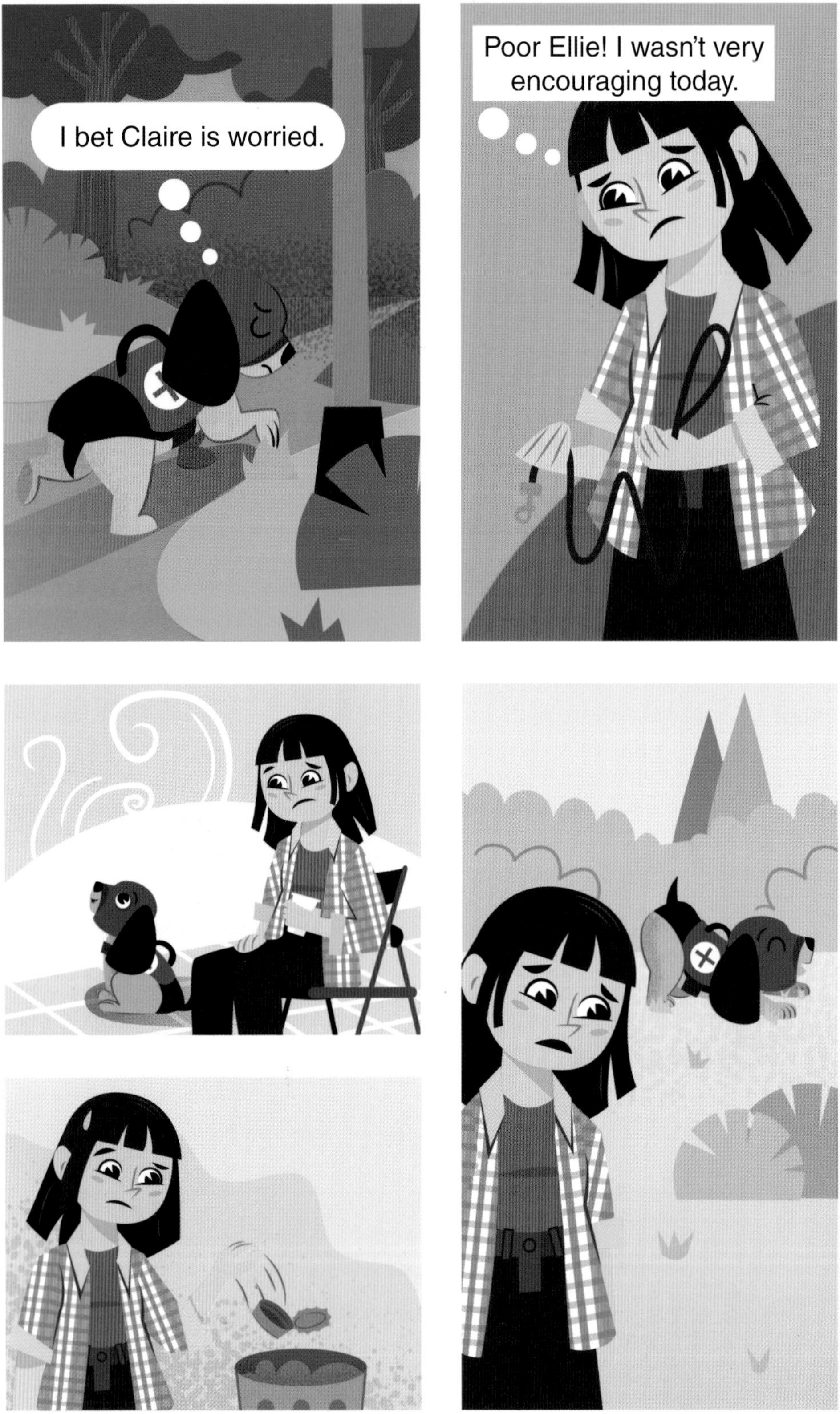
I bet Claire is worried.
Poor Ellie! I wasn't very encouraging today.

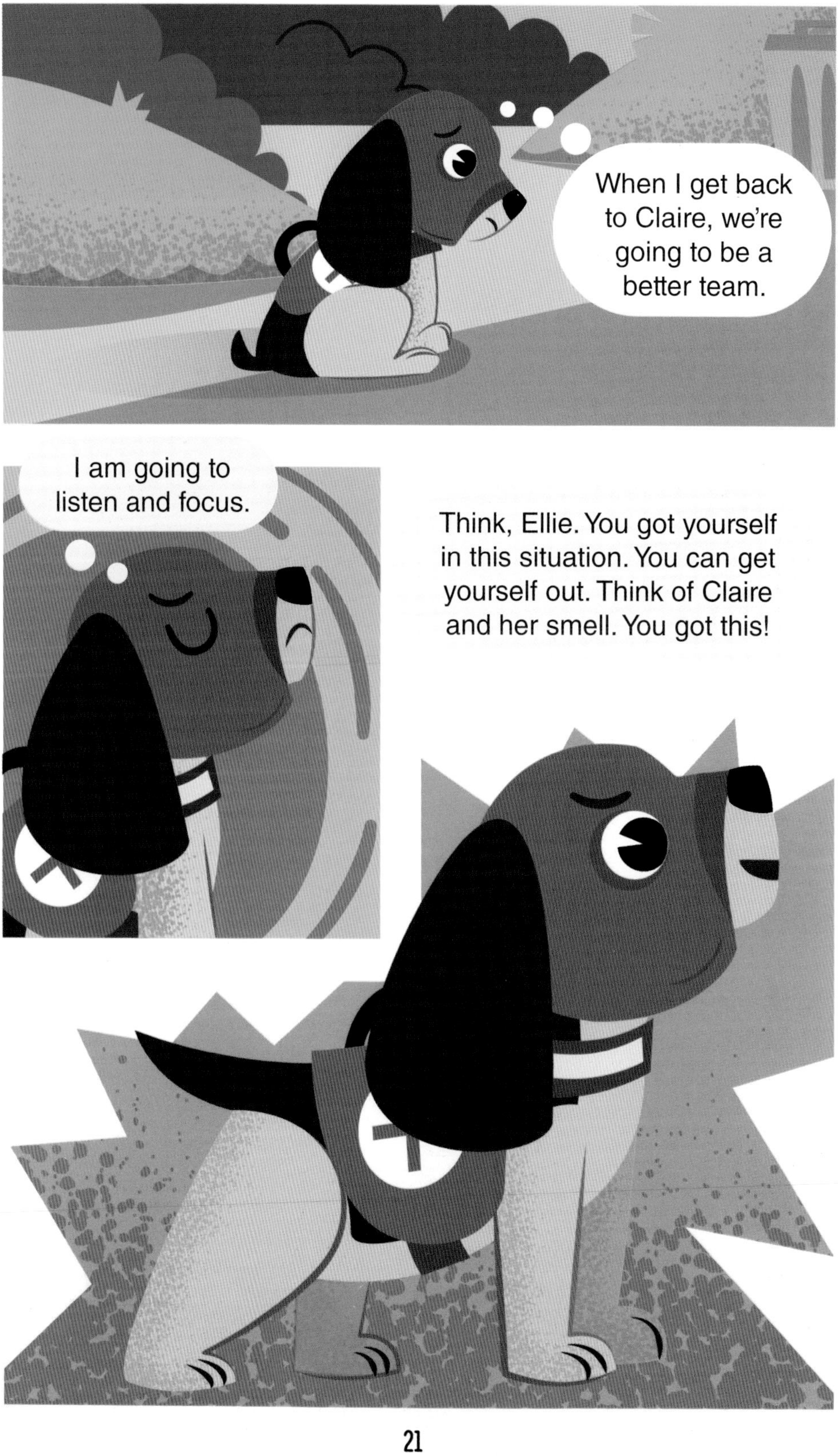
When I get back to Claire, we're going to be a better team.
I am going to listen and focus.
Think, Ellie. You got yourself in this situation. You can get yourself out. Think of Claire and her smell. You got this!

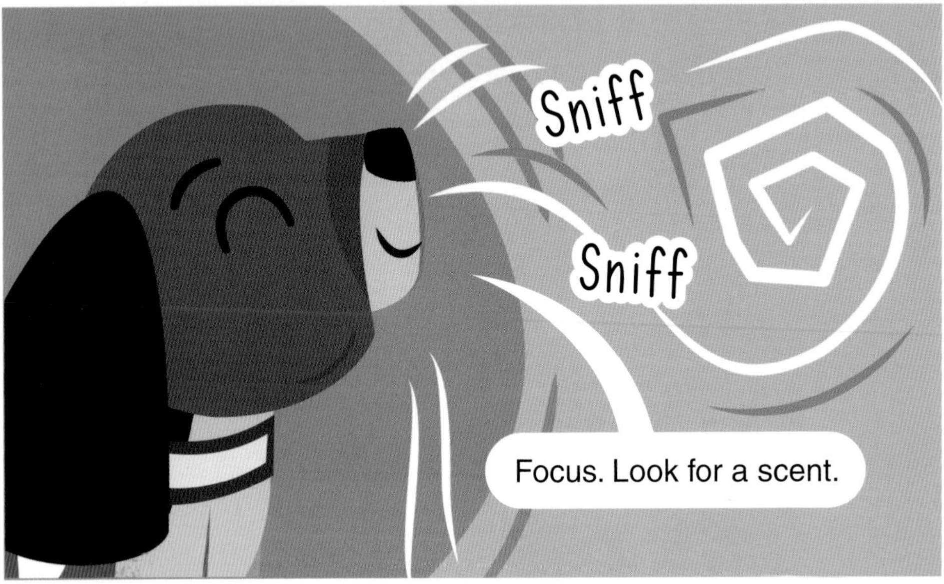
Sniff
Sniff
Focus. Look for a scent.

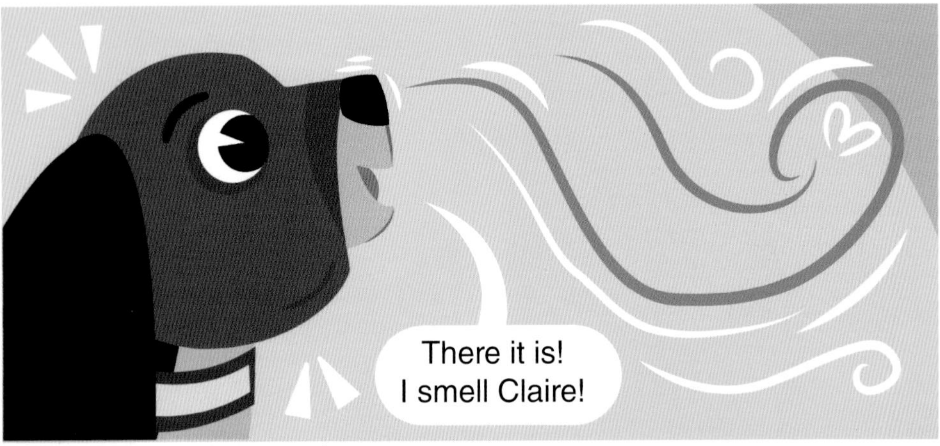
There it is!
I smell Claire!

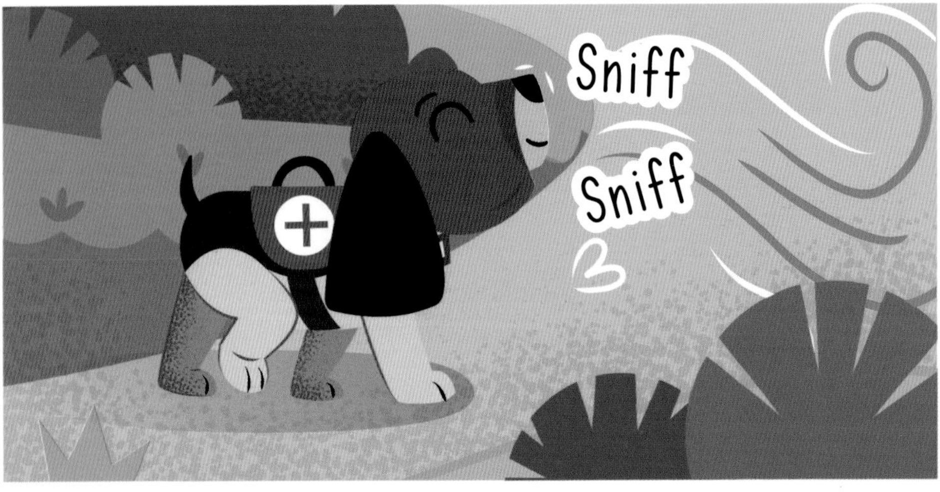
Sniff
Sniff

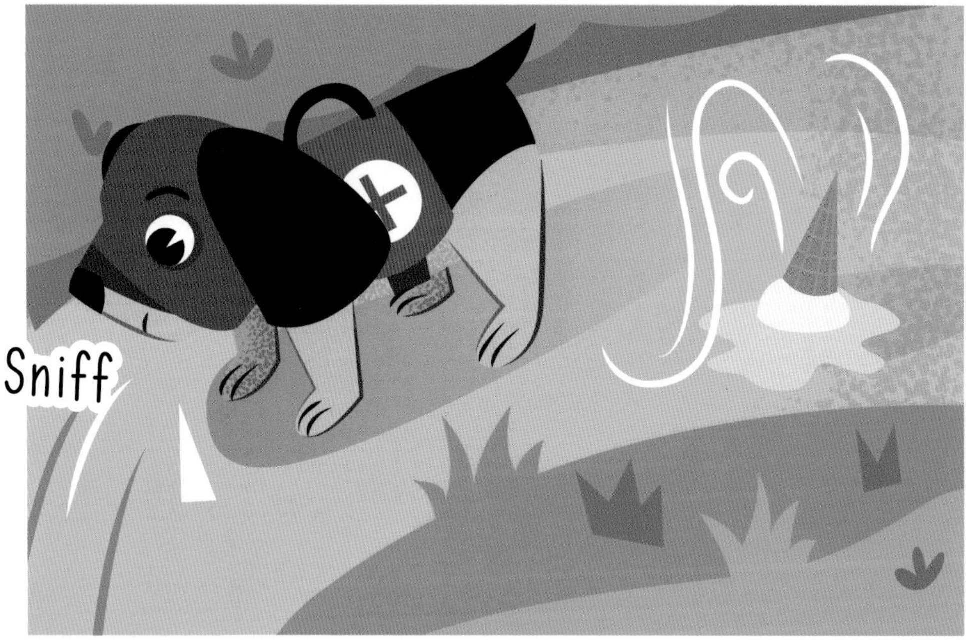
Sniff

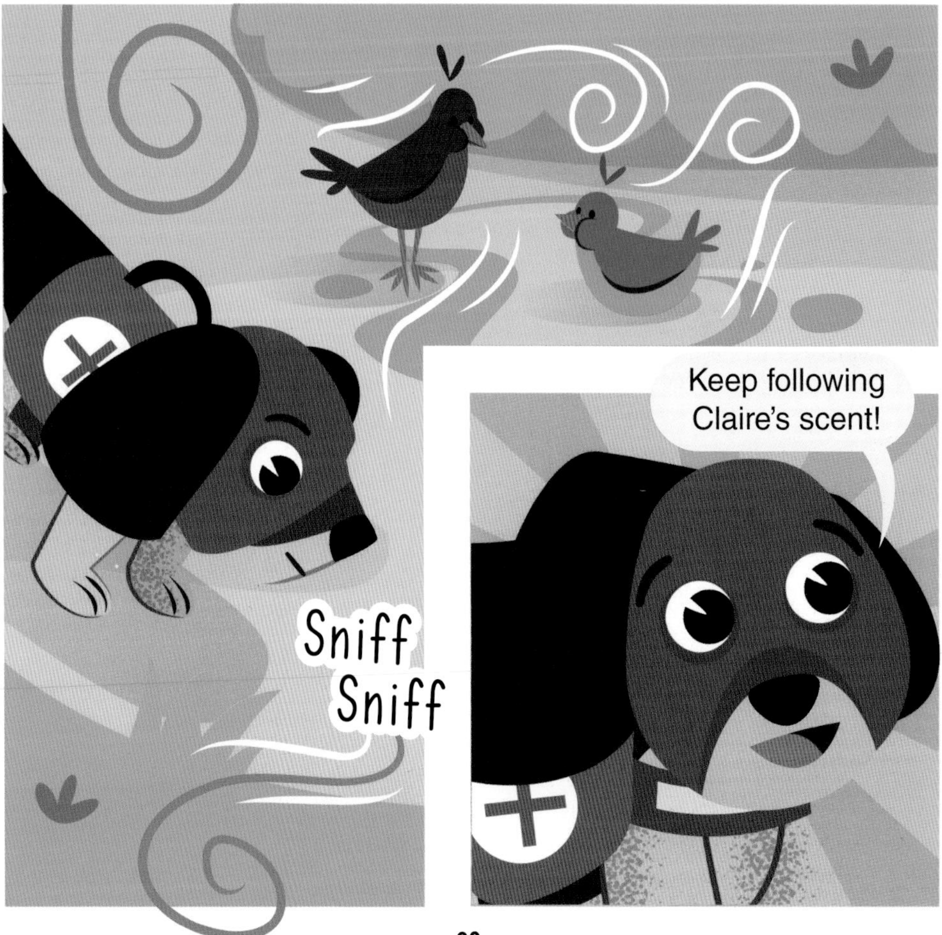
Sniff
Sniff
Keep following Claire's scent!

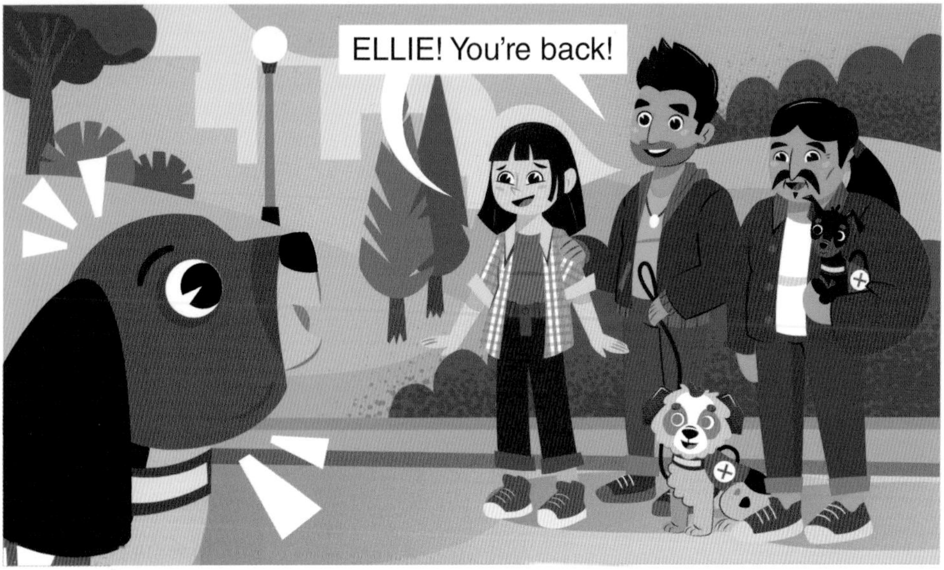
ELLIE! You're back!

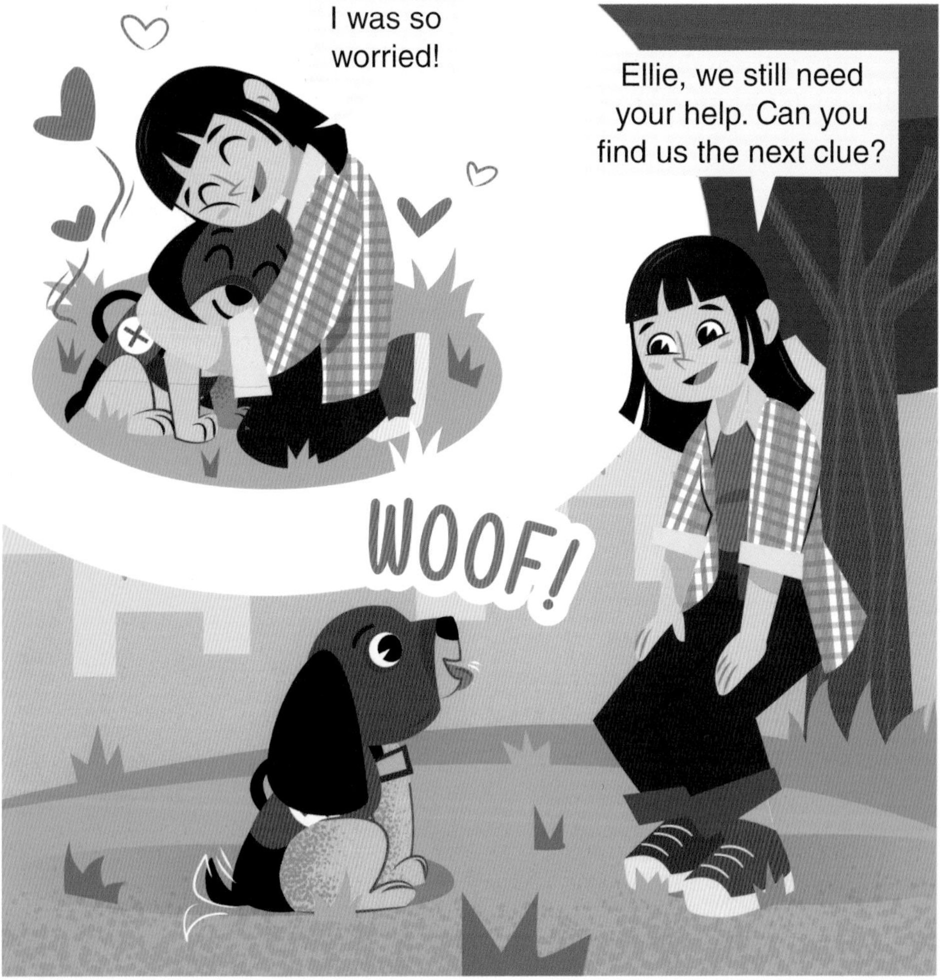
I was so worried!
Ellie, we still need your help. Can you find us the next clue?
WOOF!

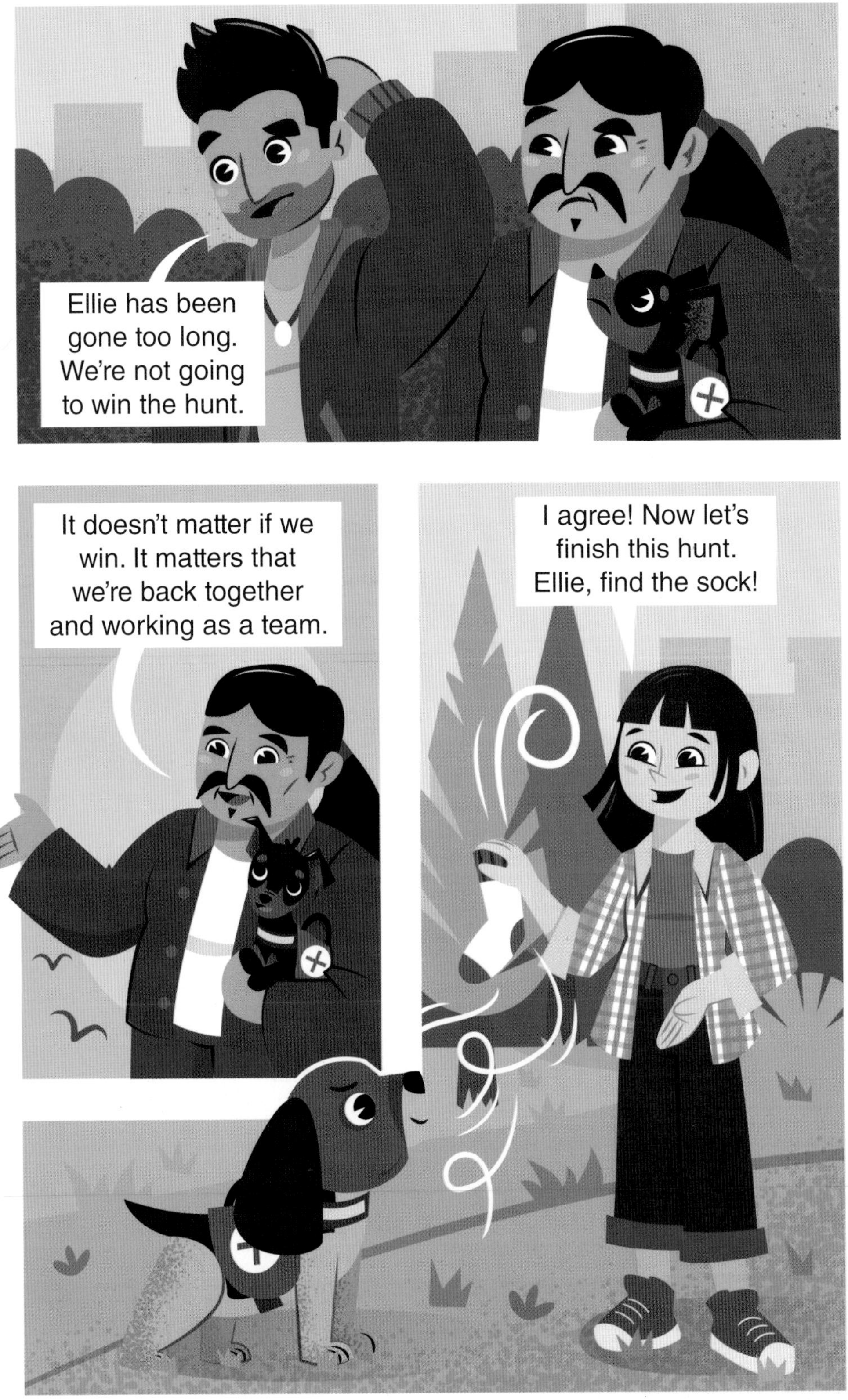
Ellie has been gone too long. We're not going to win the hunt.
It doesn't matter if we win. It matters that we're back together and working as a team.
I agree! Now let's finish this hunt. Ellie, find the sock!

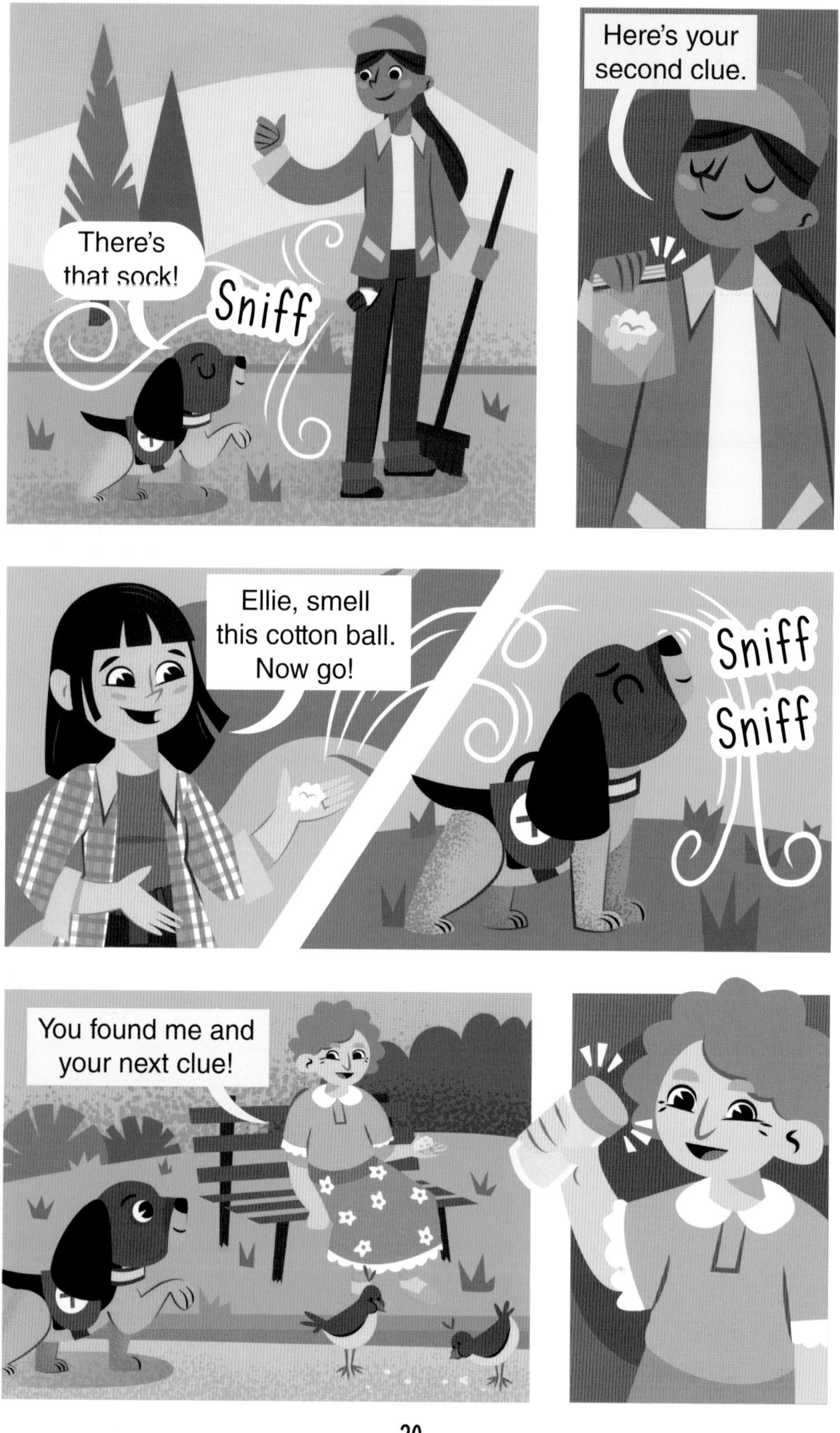
There's that sock!
Sniff
Here's your second clue.
Ellie, smell this cotton ball. Now go!
Sniff
Sniff
You found me and your next clue!

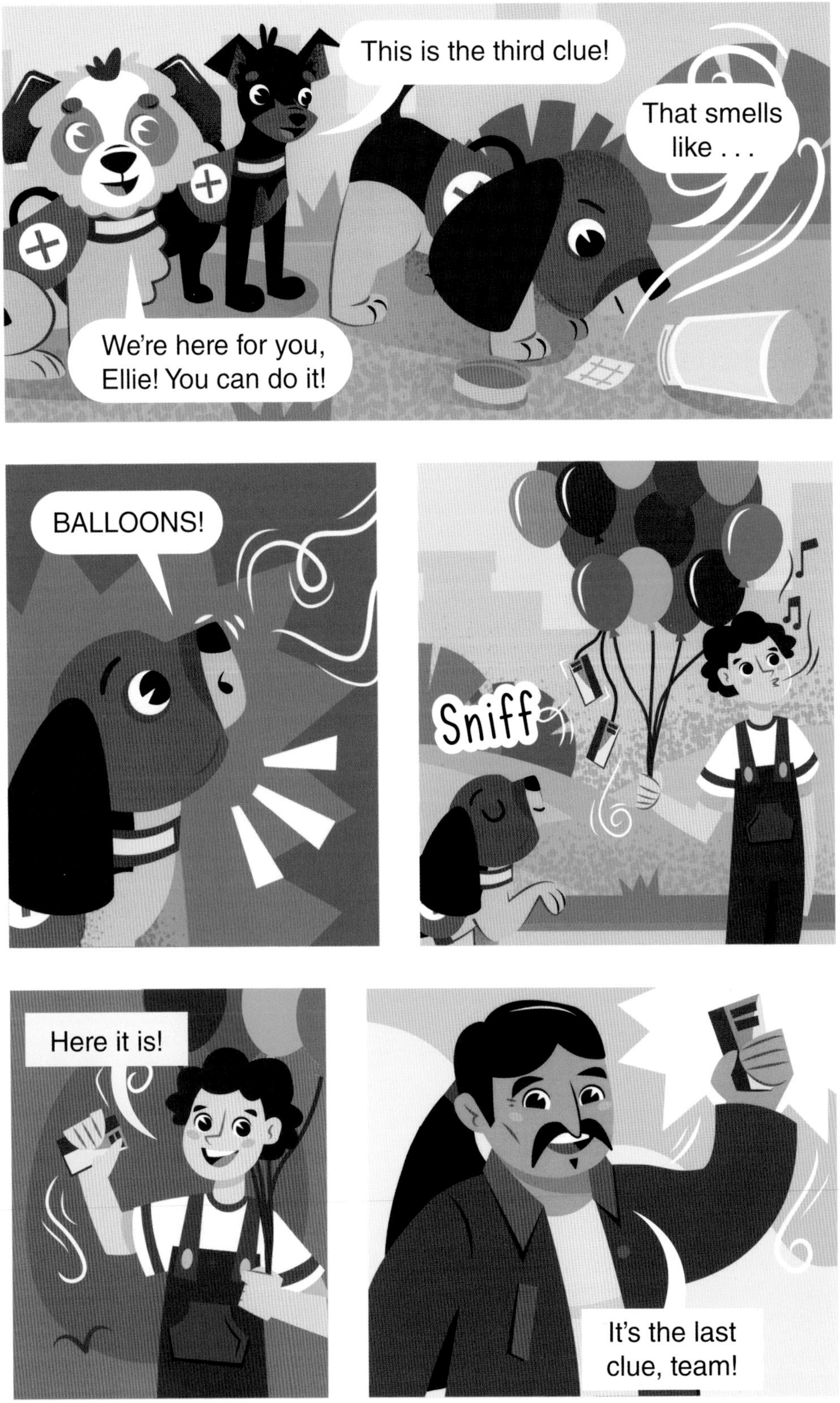

This is the third clue!
That smells like . . .
We're here for you, Ellie! You can do it!
BALLOONS!
Sniff
Here it is!
It's the last clue, team!

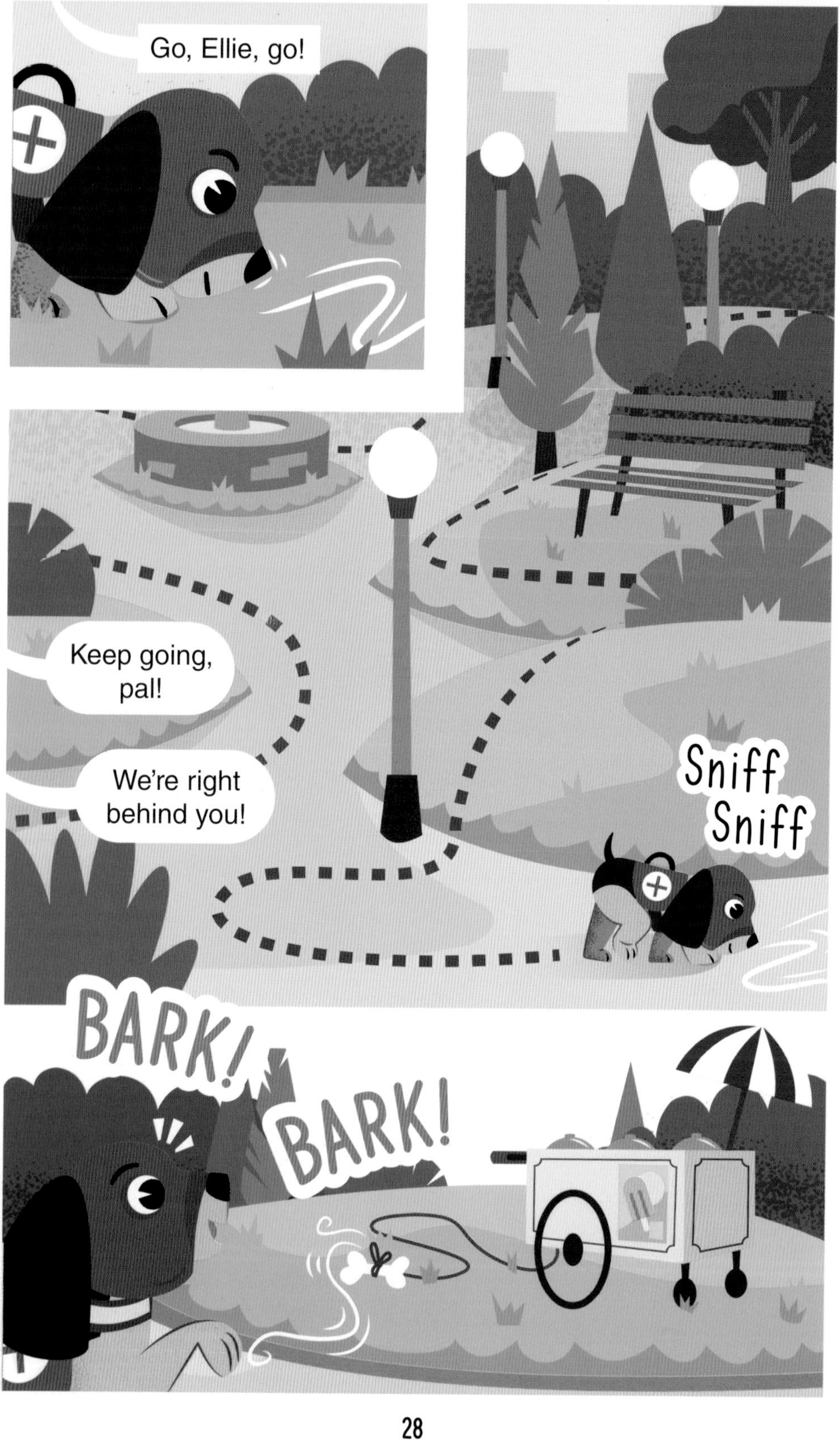
Go, Ellie, go!
Keep going, pal!
We're right behind you!
Sniff Sniff
BARK!
BARK!

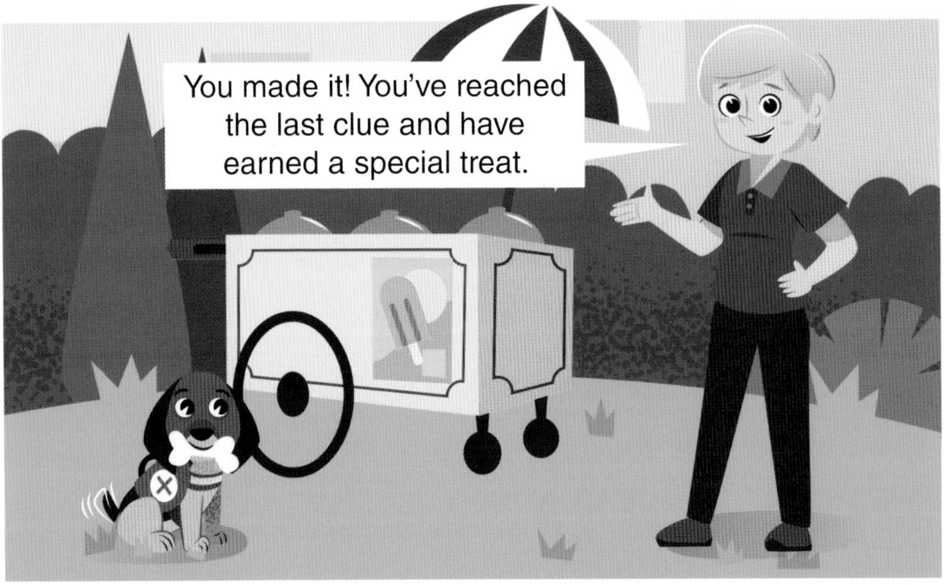
You made it! You've reached the last clue and have earned a special treat.

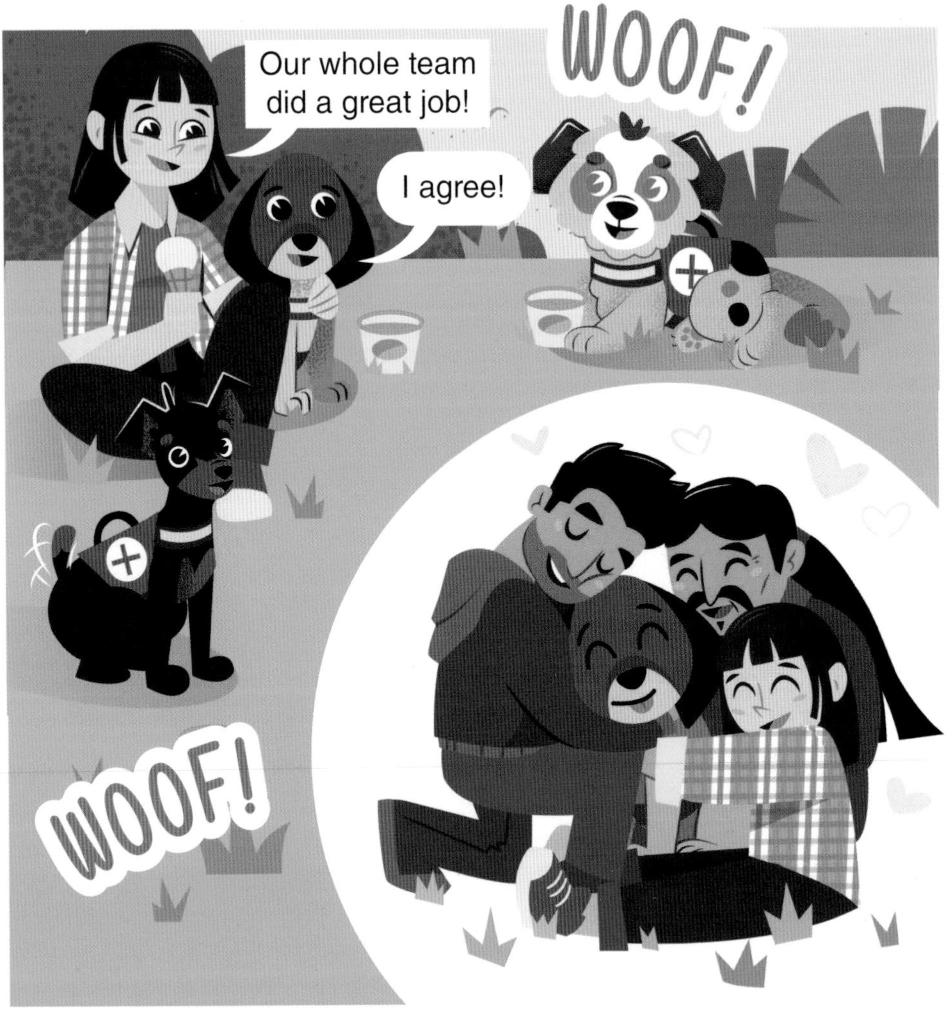
Our whole team did a great job!
WOOF!
I agree!
WOOF!

# Search & Rescue (SAR) Dogs

Search and rescue (SAR) dogs help find missing people. Sometimes, a person might be lost in the woods. Or they may be trapped under buildings, mud, snow, or water. SAR dogs can help save them.

SAR dogs can pick up a scent in the air from a half mile (0.8 kilometer) away or more! Some dogs search with their noses on the ground. They follow scents that people leave behind as they move. Air-scent dogs follow smells carried on air currents. They find where the scent originates and lead their handlers there.

Any dog can be a SAR dog, but some breeds are more skilled than others. Hunting and herding breeds, like labs, German shepherds, and border collies are often used. Bloodhounds can follow a scent for miles. Their long ears and jowls drag on the ground and stir up scents. Bloodhounds are athletic too

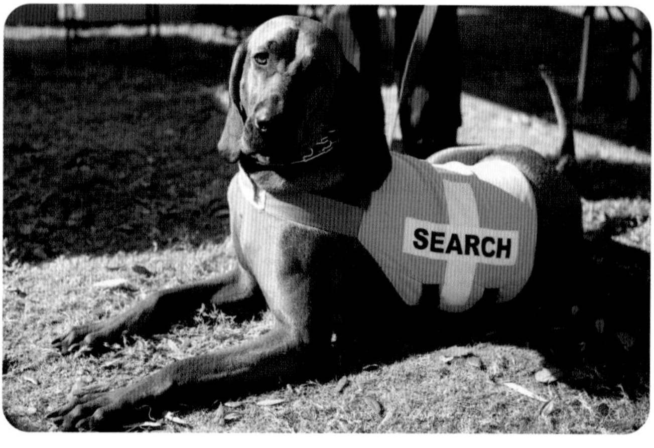
SEARCH

# Thinking About the Story

1. What is a skill or ability you are good at? Have you ever felt pressure to do it perfectly every time?

2. Ellie has a hard time focusing on her tasks. What are some things you do to help you focus?

3. How do you think Claire felt when she lost Ellie? How do you think the other pups felt?

4. Ellie is part of a team. Why is teamwork important? Do you prefer teamwork or working alone?

## About the Author

Mari Bolte is an author and editor of children's books. She lives in southern Minnesota in a house in the woods. Dogs, cats, horses, and plenty of wildlife are always nearby. Mari has worked on books on all sorts of subjects, but animal books are always the best.

## About the Illustrator

Diego Vaisberg is from Argentina. He is the DGPH Studio art director, working as designer and illustrator. He also works in the product and design department for Ink-co kids accessories brand and has been a professor in the Editorial design and Illustration Department at the Palermo University, Buenos Aires, since 2014.

## Other Books in this Series

SERVICE PUPS in Training
DAPHNE SHOWS SUPPORT
An Emotional Support Dog Graphic Novel
K9 ACADEMY
written by Mari Bolte
illustrated by Alan Brown

SERVICE PUPS in Training
ROSSI GUIDES THE WAY
A Guide Dog Graphic Novel
K9 ACADEMY
written by Mari Bolte
illustrated by Alan Brown

SERVICE PUPS in Training
TUCKER'S NOSE KNOWS
An Allergen Detection Dog Graphic Novel
K9 ACADEMY
written by Mari Bolte
illustrated by Diego Vaisberg

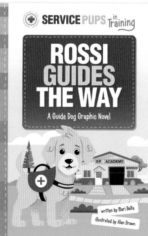